Loose Ends

Also by Electa Rome Parks

The Ties That Bind

Electa Rome Parks

New American Library

New American Library
Published by New American Library, a division of
Penguin Group (USA) Inc., 375 Hudson Street,
New York, New York 10014, USA
Penguin Group (Canada), 10 Alcorn Avenue, Toronto,
Ontario M4V 3B2, Canada (a division of Pearson Penguin Canada Inc.)
Penguin Books Ltd., 80 Strand, London WC2R 0RL, England
Penguin Ireland, 25 St. Stephen's Green, Dublin 2,
Ireland (a division of Penguin Books Ltd.)
Penguin Group (Australia), 250 Camberwell Road, Camberwell, Victoria 3124,
Australia (a division of Pearson Australia Group Pty. Ltd.)
Penguin Books India Pvt. Ltd., 11 Community Centre, Panchsheel Park,
New Delhi - 110 017, India
Penguin Group (NZ), Cnr Airborne and Rosedale Roads, Albany,
Auckland 1310, New Zealand (a division of Pearson New Zealand Ltd.)
Penguin Books (South Africa) (Pty.) Ltd., 24 Sturdee Avenue,
Rosebank, Johannesburg 2196, South Africa

Penguin Books Ltd., Registered Offices: 80 Strand, London WC2R 0RL, England

Published by New American Library, a division of Penguin Group (USA) Inc. Originally published by Xlibris Corporation.

Copyright © Electa Rome Parks, 2002
Readers Guide copyright © Penguin Group (USA) Inc., 2004
All rights reserved

Cover image credits:
Top image: © Matthew Alan/CORBIS. Middle image: © Digital Vision/Gettyone. Bottom image: © Elizabeth Young/Gettyone.

(NAL) REGISTERED TRADEMARK—MARCA REGISTRADA

ISBN 0-7394-4787-4

Set in Bembo with Chalet
Designed by Daniel Lagin

Printed in the United States of America

It is in our lives and not our words that our religion must be read.
—Thomas Jefferson, 1743–1826

Uncle Robert, 1925–1999
In dedication to a strong, black man who lived it . . . Rest in peace.

I believe that you can do something in an instant that will give you heartache for life.   —Author Unknown

Acknowledgments

Whew! Where do I begin? This past year has been a year of self-discovery, education, and forming ties with many new and talented writers. 2003 was an amazing year! Thank you, God, for giving me a measure of talent and the faith to have the ability to follow my dreams and find my true niche in life. You've been so good to me!

To the many avid readers, bookstores and book clubs that have shown me love, praise, support and encouragement on this wonderful journey, thank you; it means more than you'll ever know. You've truly touched my heart.

Special love goes to my husband, Nelson, and our two children. You guys gave me hugs, smiles, kisses, words of encouragement and, most of all, the space, peace and quiet to complete this project. In my household, that's almost a miracle (smile).

Thanks to Tresseler Rome for her constant feedback and for always asking, "When are you going to finish that book? What's going to happen to . . . ?" In your own way, you proved you were proud of your big sister. Remember when we were small and I called you Tress the Pest (LOL)? This is your year, 2004.

To Laymon Taylor, DaJuan Crooms and Jordan Rome, thanks for playing a major role in my life. Your being here comforts my soul. Betty Rakestraw, you always go the extra mile. Sonya Morris and family, I know I can always call on you.

To other family members and friends (you know who you are), thanks for accepting me . . . for me. Buffie Stroud and Audrey

Thomas, I appreciate and embrace the kind words of love and support.

Sharron Nuckles, you've been here from day one and you're still here. That says it all. Remember Columbia, S.C., and the house party? Girl, I'm still laughing. Thanks for being a true measure of real friendship. Plus, you know all my secrets (LOL).

Special thanks to my agent, Marc Gerald, and editor Janete Scobie for making everything run smoothly and providing a seamless transition into mainstream publishing. I couldn't have done it without you. You guys are godsends.

Mardessa Smith, of Jadis Communications, Inc., thanks for helping me take it to another level. You didn't know pep talks were part of your package, did you? I told you I met you for a reason . . . I'm still waiting to do lunch.

Thanks go out to my network of writing buddies. I've learned so much from you guys. Thanks for keeping it real: Hope C. Clarke, Magdalene Breaux, Sybil Barkley-Staples, Tim Everett and Clark Kent. Keep hope alive!

I have to shout out a few bookstores: Marcus Williams at Nubian, Fanta at Oasis, Nzenga at African Spectrum and Nia at Medu Bookstore, thanks for opening your doors and your hearts and allowing me an opportunity to reach my wonderful readers.

Shout-outs to the following book clubs: Shani Book Club, Obsidian Book Club, I'm on My Way Book Club, Sister 2 Sister Book Club and It's a She Thang Book Club, thanks for your gracious hospitality and support.

Shout-outs to Rawsistaz, Sharon Hudson, Disilgold, A Nu Twista Flava, *SORMAG,* Alvin Romer, *Booking Matters* magazine, Wetaugust, APOO, Literary World, Flavah Reviewers, the Nubian Chronicles, Lori Holman (my number one fan) and TNC Reviews for providing a positive medium for the writing community.

Signing off in Atlanta, Georgia. Remember, the only place where your dream becomes impossible is in your own thinking. I think

I'll go and write for a while. . . . I have this wonderful idea for a story about this woman who . . . Stay tuned. Peace and many blessings.

Much love,

Electa
March 2004

Loose Ends

Prologue

I had the dream—or should I say nightmare—again last night. It was terrifying, as usual. I awoke with my thin white top drenched in sweat, my heart pounding away a mile a minute. In the dream I was fast asleep, lying on my back, totally nude, and *he* was straddling me.

When he awakened me from my sleep, roughly kissing me on my partially open lips and placing his hot, urgent tongue inside my mouth, I realized he was someone I should fear. At first I opened my mouth to scream, but then I looked into his brown eyes and they possessed me, hypnotized me with their power. It was as if he were looking into my soul—and I was lost.

I couldn't fight him. I slowly opened my trembling legs and he entered me with a savage fury. It was as if his very existence depended upon conquering my womanhood. Unbelievably, I desperately wanted him inside me, and my already moist walls eagerly accepted his ever-expanding manhood. His hungry mouth devoured my throbbing nipples, right as I was on the brink of sheer ecstasy. He pounded away at a frantic pace, his large hands encircling my neck and squeezing with all his might as he cried out, "Why, tell me why did you betray me?" Then I woke up . . . gasping for breath.

I believe that no matter how bad your heart is broken, the
world doesn't stop for your grief.   —Author Unknown

The nightmares . . . they started again; it had been almost a year
since the last one. Twelve peaceful months in which I almost,
just almost, forgot the sheer terror of seeing *him* towering over me
like some unstoppable, superhuman force. One year in which I felt
normal and whole again because I had finally cleansed him from my
system, from my soul.

Him being my ex-husband, Brice. It was still hard to get my
mouth and mind to speak his name again. Speaking his name
brought up too many memories, memories that I didn't want to deal
with, memories that I couldn't deal with yet. And it has been five
years since our divorce. Brice, the man I thought was my soul mate
in life, my black knight in shining armor, the love of my life, the man
of my dreams. The man I gave my heart, mind and body to, willingly and unselfishly. Brice soon became more like the man of my
nightmares.

The nightmares were so real, for a few minutes when I was between being asleep and waking up, I thought I was still with him. He
still possessed me, and it scared me to death. Brice used to beat the
shit out of me, whenever he wanted to, just because he could. Brice
controlled me totally. Brice was a man who would lay down the law,
his law, and expect me to follow it . . . or else.

I'm embarrassed to say that it took me a while to end it. No, I
didn't enjoy getting my butt beaten or being treated like a child by a
man who screwed me whenever and however he wanted to after he

beat my ass. I stayed because I thought he would change, that my love would make him change. And yes, I loved him with all my heart and soul. It took a trip to the hospital for me to wake up, literally, and see the light before it was too late. Still, he took a part of me that I could never get back. You see, he took my heart.

They say life is full of paradoxes. How could you both love and hate someone? I didn't know, but I did. As crazy as it might sound, a part of me would always love him. A part of me would always belong to Brice. That's sick, isn't it?

I couldn't ask for a better life now. In fact, I have been blessed with a wonderful husband, Christian, who adores me; I know that for a fact. Christian was Brice's best friend. Actually, they were more like brothers. It's all so complicated. The ties that bind. Christian gave up everything for me. I know; my life read like a soap opera. Now I'm mostly drama free.

Anyway, Christian and I have been married for three and a half, almost four years. It's been wonderful; our marriage is everything I never had with Brice. I love my husband so much! When Christian makes love to me, I feel it in his touch, his eyes and his soft, whispered words. We have a beautiful two-year-old daughter named Lyric. We named her Lyric because she brings joy and harmony into our lives. She has a head full of hair and green eyes just like her daddy. Yeah, life couldn't be better. This is the family I have dreamed of all my life.

If only the nightmares would stop. That way, I wouldn't have to see him again. And then I could forget.

As I lay on my back, stared at the cream-colored ceiling and made a mental checklist of the things I needed to do around the house the next day, I turned over onto my left side and smiled at my husband, Christian, asleep with not a care in the world. I could watch him sleep all night. Christian is such a handsome man and he's all mine. I'm not being boastful; I'm just keeping it real.

He's paper-bag brown, a few inches over six feet tall and roughly

225 pounds of pure man. Christian has the sexiest pair of green eyes, bedroom eyes. With his broad shoulders and iron-board stomach, for a man thirty-eight years old his body could easily pass for that of a twenty-eight-year-old. His looks aren't why I love him so; I love him because of his heart. It's wide-open for me.

An hour earlier Christian had shown me how much he loved me in his own special way. Just thinking about that gave me goose bumps up and down my arms and a familiar tingling between my legs.

Tonight was date night! At least once a month, Christian and I set aside one night, a Friday or Saturday, to do something together, just the two of us. Christian and I had only been together a little over a year and a half when we had Lyric.

Anyway, date night didn't have to be anything extravagant. Usually it was something simple, like going to the movies. I love horror flicks. There's something about all that blood and gore. I know, call me bizarre. Sometimes we go dancing at one of the hot spots in Midtown or out for a nice dinner in Buckhead.

Christian and I took Lyric over to Mama's house for the night, where she's spoiled beyond reason. Lyric loves her grandmother to death and vice versa. I'm so proud of Mama. She has gotten her life back on track after a bout with alcoholism that lasted for years. That's another story in itself. AA, the twelve-step program and a strong will have made a big difference in Mama's life.

This evening, Christian had everything planned the minute I unlocked the door and walked into our stucco home from a hard day at work. It had been a busy day—a busy week—at Fairfield Elementary School. I am a third-grade schoolteacher to a bunch of hyperactive, rambunctious but adorable students . . . my children. However, at the end of the week I am ready to relax and unwind with my handsome husband. In our sunken living room, I was greeted with kisses by both Lyric and Christian. Lyric was finishing up her snack of graham crackers and Christian was cleaning up the trail of crumbs that followed behind her.

As I slowly undressed and stepped into the fragrant, lilac-scented bubble bath he had waiting for me in our garden tub, Christian drove

Lyric over to Mama's house about seven miles away. He had placed candles around the tub, with light jazz playing softly in the background. With a glass of my favorite white wine in hand, I lay back and closed my tired eyes as I immersed myself up to my neck in bubbles. I could feel the tension drifting away inch by inch. I was in seventh heaven and must have dozed off briefly, because I suddenly awakened when I heard Christian moving around in our bedroom. As I prepared myself to step out of the bathtub, Christian came in with a big white fluffy bath towel and dried me off so erotically that I didn't want him to stop.

Slowly, he led me into our bedroom with passionate kisses. More candles had been lit, illuminating the room. Christian placed me gently on our king-size bed with the burgundy comforter and rubbed me down in my favorite Victoria's Secret body oil. In between massages, we exchanged warm, deep-tongued kisses and loving caresses. Christian and I didn't take it any further; we had all night to savor each other. The night was still young.

After I dressed in one of my sexy, see-through black negligees that Christian simply adores, he brought in a small tray of fruit, cheese, crackers and more wine that had chilled in the refrigerator. He took a quick hot shower and we spent the remainder of the night watching old movies rented from Blockbuster, snacking and cuddling. I could watch *Sparkle* and *Cooley High* over and over again. They are true classics.

We had dessert around midnight, when he pulled off my gown with his teeth and seductively kissed me from the top of my head to the bottom of my toes, taking his time to appreciate all of me, inch by inch. Christian knows every mole, nook and cranny on my body. He is in tune with my body. The climax of the evening was when he buried his head between my parted thighs and feasted until I begged him to enter me.

I glanced over at the green numbers on the digital clock that sat on our cherry-wood nightstand and noticed it was almost two A.M. The last few nights I had insomnia. I guess it was my body's way of rebelling against the nightmares. I was too afraid to sleep. Most evenings, I read and watched Christian sleep, like tonight.

I reached over to caress his cheek and he turned in my direction. Instinctively, Christian pulled me to him in our spooning position. As he held me in his semitight embrace, I could feel his love radiating warmth throughout my body.

"Mia, you still up?" he asked in a sexy, sleepy voice. "What time is it?"

"Yes, I'm about to go to sleep. I just finished reading my *Essence* magazine. Go back to sleep; it's almost two A.M."

His warm hand traveled to my right breast and gently squeezed. I let out a soft moan. "First tell me who's the man?" he asked.

"Boo, you know you are." I smiled at this familiar game we always played.

His hand traced an imaginary line down my taut stomach, stopped and dipped between my thighs and gently rubbed. "Let me hear you say it."

"Baby, you the man! You own my stuff. It has your name stamped all over it. You have copyright papers," I said in the most serious tone I could manage.

"You know that, and don't you ever forget it or I'll have to prove it to you again." Christian snuggled closer to me and nuzzled my neck.

There was a comfortable silence as we appreciated the moment and our closeness in the early-morning hours.

Christian spoke gently into the darkness. "I love you, baby. You and Lyric are my world."

"I love you more," I declared, lifting my right hand to caress his cheek.

"Promise me you'll never leave me." His silliness returned. "I love you so much, I'd drink your bathwater," he shrieked in his best Chris Tucker imitation.

"Yeah, yeah, whatever, man," I said, giggling. As we laughed again, Christian pulled me closer into his safe embrace and we slowly drifted into our own separate slumbers.

Christian

I believe that no matter how good a friend is, they're going to hurt you every once in a while, and you must forgive them for that. —Author Unknown

After sleeping in until nearly eleven, Mia and I finally ate a light brunch of ham-and-turkey sandwiches, fruit, chips and iced tea. I haven't slept in that late in a while. I usually rise with the sun. It's true what they say: Old habits are hard to break. You see, I'm ex-military, and rising early and putting in several hours of hard work had been drilled into me at a very early age. I was discharged from the marines a few months before I married Mia, my one true love. I didn't want to bring her back into that environment again for various reasons.

Now my full-time occupation is being a loving and devoted husband and a doting father, and working as head of security at a financial institution in Midtown. There, I work everything from first to third shift, usually rotating my schedule. I like a hands-on approach; I like to know my staff, and found this way allowed me to accomplish that.

After I walked Mia out to her black Ford Explorer, opened the driver's door for her, gave her a quick kiss on the cheek, and watched as she drove off to pick up Lyric, I silently wondered again what was bothering her. I know my wife all too well, and something was definitely on Mia's mind. She still had dark circles under her eyes like she didn't sleep a wink. Mia did a lot of tossing and turning again last night. And a few times I even heard her call out softly in a fretful sleep, but I couldn't understand what she was saying. I wrapped my arms protectively around her and eventually she calmed back down.

These dreams have been going on for roughly two, three weeks at the most, and Mia refuses to talk about them. I'm positive I know the subject of her dreams—Brice, her ex-husband and my ex-best friend. Mia hasn't seen him in over five years. The last time Mia set eyes on him was in the midst of a violent fight, when he was beating her ass and she ended up in the hospital.

It's been almost that long for me as well. A few months later, Brice and I had a confrontation before his departure overseas with the marines. I guess back then we were both running from our own internal demons. Brice chose to run to another country; I chose to remove myself from the source of my pain and bittersweet memories. That time frame and period in my life seems like light-years ago. The person I was back then doesn't even exist anymore.

It's a long story the way Mia and I got together. My wife is a lovely thirty-year-old lady with beautiful brown eyes, high cheekbones, a head of thick, black, wavy hair that she keeps short and a petite body that won't quit. I love her with all my heart and soul. I could be in a room full of supermodels or even Janet Jackson or Halle Berry and I'd still have eyes only for my Mia. Well, maybe I'd look, but I'd have love for only Mia. And that's saying a lot, since I am a retired player.

A few years ago, if someone told me I would be married with a two-year-old daughter, I would have laughed in his face. Back then, women had only one thing I needed. I'm the first one to admit that I loved myself some beautiful black women. God knew exactly what he was doing when he made these wonderful, sexy, sensual creatures He called women. Whisper a few sweet words in their ears, treat them like they're special, even if only for that moment, and they take you to heaven and back.

Women don't realize just how much power they possess between their legs. Men don't want to admit it, but women have the power, and some of them have figured that truth out. There's nothing like the feel or touch of a woman's silky body against a masculine one, and when a man takes her to ecstasy, makes her come, it's an amazing feeling. Men never get enough. Unfortunately for me, I was making the trip to heaven every opportunity I received from every and any driver I could find.

Then Mia came into my life via Brice and all that changed. Mia changed my world as I knew it. She has brought so much joy into my life; if only she would learn to trust and share her feelings and thoughts with me. Mia keeps everything bottled up so tightly it's amazing she doesn't explode. I understand some of her reasons, because I know how she was raised and some of the things that have happened in her lifetime. But . . . I want Mia to know and believe that I'm not going to hurt her, mentally or physically. It saddens me to think that she would ever doubt my love for her.

Sometimes, I think Mia is looking for the moment when I will hit her. That will never happen. Mia is very headstrong and we've had some pretty heated arguments, but I'd cut off my right arm before I'd strike her.

I know these nightmares are all stemming from what I made the mistake of telling her about a month ago. It was a lazy Sunday afternoon. Mia and I were stretched out, as usual, on the sofa in the living room half watching some old Western movie on TV. Lyric was fast asleep, taking her midday nap, with her favorite baby doll and stuffed bear nearby.

Mia's arms were wrapped around my waist, her head on my chest, half dozing. I looked down at her for a moment and caressed her face. "Baby, you're not going to believe who wrote me the other day."

"Who?" she asked sleepily, readjusting her head on my chest.

"You'll never guess in your wildest dreams."

"I don't know, who?" she asked again. "I give up."

I paused for only a second. This was going to be a shock for Mia, as it had been for me as well.

"Brice, Brice Matthew."

Mia didn't say anything at first, but I felt her body stiffen beside me and now she was fully awake. She finally spoke with a slight shakiness in her voice. "What do you mean, he wrote you? How did he get our address?"

"He wrote me in care of his cousin Reggie. You know I run into Reggie now and then over at the gym where he works part-time. Don't worry; Brice doesn't know where we live, baby."

Mia didn't say anything as she stared into space with a strange expression. She had raised herself up from my embrace and was glaring down at me. I continued on.

"In the letter, Brice was talking about letting bygones be bygones and righting his wrongs. To make a long story short, Brice wants to meet with us. He and his wife, Kree, returned to the States about three months ago."

Mia pulled herself up further with one elbow and was looking down at me with this frantic, scared expression on her face.

"Mia, I don't know. I would like for us to meet . . ."

"What do you mean? You mean you are considering it?" she asked in an urgent, frightened tone.

"Mia, listen, I know you don't like to think about Brice and that time in your life. But baby, you need to put closure, final closure, to that." I softly rubbed her back over and over, up and down. We sat in complete silence for a few seconds. I witnessed the mixed emotions in her facial expression.

"I've put closure to that period. I don't want to see him *or* his new wife. And I don't understand why you would either, Christian. You know all the shit that man put me through. I don't need your Psychology 101 speech and analysis."

"Baby, he can't hurt you now. You've got me; I got your back. Mia, don't you see this could be a way for you—"

"Christian, I'm absolutely not going to meet with him, and you can't make me. I can't believe you'd ask me to. I can't believe this . . . You do what you want to, but he'd better not come near me or Lyric," she screamed as she jumped up, ran into our bedroom and slammed the door so hard that one of our framed prints fell off the wall in the hallway.

I thought to myself that a silent storm was approaching.

Brice

I believe that it isn't always enough to be forgiven by others. Sometimes you have to learn to forgive yourself.
—Author Unknown

I absently rubbed Kree's ass, exposed in all its glory. I pulled the navy satin sheet down while she continued to sleep peacefully. Good sex always put her to sleep afterward, and I always gave her good loving. The more I leaned back against my pillow, caressing her between the legs and staring at her sleeping, the more aroused I became. Kree, at twenty-five years old, is a stunning woman with long, thick black hair, big light brown eyes with long eyelashes, high cheekbones with glowing, medium-brown skin, long legs and full, kissable lips.

I met Kree my second year in Germany. We met at a club I had heard great things about and was checking out for the first time. She was on the lit dance floor strutting her stuff to the music when I arrived. After ordering a beer, I walked away from the crowded bar and sat down at a vacant table that gave me a great view of her.

I watched Kree from a short distance. She appeared to get lost in the song and was a great dancer. Kree was so sensual and sexy; it was like she was making love to the music. The way she would close her eyes for a few seconds, lick her full lips and throw her head back was erotic. Kree had on a sexy black dress that fit every curve, no accessories except for a pair of diamond-stud earrings and a pair of black spike-heeled shoes. I didn't see a panty line, so I was pretty sure she didn't have on any underwear.

At one point, when she glanced toward the bar, our eyes met and locked. I smiled. Kree smiled shyly in my direction and quickly turned away. Afterward, I saw her glance back at me once or twice.

I drank a few more beers and mostly people-watched. No other woman had captured my attention the way the lady in black had. I'm sure I could have talked to any woman in the dark club, the way I kept getting the eye from several of them. Back then, after thirty-four years of living, I knew when a woman was attracted to me, and that night I was getting vibes left and right.

I was dressed casually, not in marine gear, and noticed the women checking me out, some boldly and some on the sly. There were several pretty women in the club who wouldn't have objected to leaving with me for a night of dancing between the sheets. But I was interested in the lady in black; she reminded me of someone. I couldn't put my finger on it. Kree appeared so innocent, yet sexy and so beautiful.

Finally a slow song came on. I placed my beer on the table and made my way through the crowd of people exiting the dance floor. I located Kree attempting to leave as well. I walked up to her, took her hand and told her to dance with me. She did.

Hours later, tucked away in our own private booth, I discovered that Kree was a twenty-one-year-old, American-born college student. Kree was an army brat. Her parents had traveled all over the world, thanks to the United States Army. During her last year in high school, Kree's father was transferred to Germany. She had fallen in love with the country, and when they left she stayed behind to attend college.

Kree and I talked for most of that night and early into the next morning. I remember we were one of the last to leave the club. Her girlfriends left long before, after I had promised to get Kree safely home, and after assuring them that I wasn't a rapist or on an *America's Most Wanted* list.

I decided Kree was actually kinda shy. I think I intimidated her a little. However, I was getting strong vibes that she was attracted to me. I decided to see how far I could go with her. At one point I reached under the table and caressed her thigh through the sheer, flimsy fabric of her black dress. Kree looked at me with those big eyes, but didn't protest. I kept looking into her eyes, telling her how beautiful she was. She smiled. The entire time I was pulling the hem of her dress up to reach under with my hand.

Just like I thought, Kree didn't have on any underwear. I rubbed my hand up and down her smooth leg, but decided to back off and take it slow. For the remainder of the night, we were lost in good conversation.

As they say, the rest is history. Kree made my tour in Germany quite memorable. At some point—I'm not sure when it happened— I realized I couldn't live without her. We've been married for almost three years. Kree is a good wife; she does what I tell her to and knows I'm the man of our house. She thoroughly understands that.

Tonight I was frustrated. Usually after round two I left Kree alone. But tonight I was seriously thinking about waking her up, as I did so often, to have her go down on me. Sometimes she would protest, but usually she gave in. Kree could do that shit all too well. Or sometimes by the time she woke up I was already inside her, grinding away. Eventually she would wrap her long legs around my waist and give in to the good feelings. I'd look down at her and she'd be all into us.

Tonight my attention was focused elsewhere. I had talked to my cousin Reggie, and I knew Christian had received the short letter I had written him weeks earlier. It had taken me a week to finish that letter, and now I was anxiously waiting for a response. True friendship—true brotherhood—is not something to be taken lightly. I had learned that. I did a lot of stupid shit in my past, things I did when I was younger and dumber, things I truly regretted. I wanted to right my mistakes, my regrets.

Hopefully Christian would call me soon. I had put our phone number in the letter. I admit it: I missed him. I couldn't wait to see the man who was once like a blood brother to me . . . and the lady who was my everything. At some point in his life, every man has one, the one woman he loves with everything he has. The one woman who makes him say and do shit he'd never think of doing for anyone else. Stuff he can't even believe he's doing. For me, that was Mia. No, I never forgot Mia. I still see her face in my dreams.

Kree

I believe that your life can be changed in a matter of
hours by people who don't even know you.

—Author Unknown

"Hello?"

"Where have you been?"

"Oh, hey, sweetie. What's up?" I asked, attempting to balance the
cordless phone against my right ear as I opened the oven to check on
dinner.

"Hey, baby, I'm on my way home. Where have you been?"

"Well, hello to you too," I said in mock indignation.

"Where have you been?" he impatiently asked again.

"Nowhere, baby, why? I've been here all day cleaning up, washing
and preparing your favorite meal," I stated nervously into the phone.

"Well, I called earlier, around two, and you didn't answer. The
phone rang about eight times and the answering machine wasn't on.
You never picked up. Where were you?"

"I was probably in the shower and just didn't hear the phone
ringing. Baby, I have steak, well-done just like you love it. Baked potatoes with sour cream and chives, a garden salad, all your favorites.
Hurry home before it gets cold," I said to change the subject.

"Sounds good," he said absently. "Did I get any phone calls?"

"No, none, baby."

"Damn. Okay, I'm on my way. I'll be there in about twenty minutes if this traffic isn't too bad. But rush-hour traffic being horrible
is always something you can count on in Atlanta."

"I'm starting to realize that."

"I have a really good feeling about this meeting I just left. The loan officer, Mr. Petty, was pretty cool. I think I may get the small-business loan after all. Listen, go ahead and fix my plate; I'm starving. And change into something sexy for me."

"Okay, I'll see you soon. Bye." I placed the phone back on the hook and hurried into the bathroom to take a quick shower, rub my body all over with Bath & Body Works' Lavender Flowers cream, and put on my hot-red lingerie that Brice loves to see me in. It wouldn't stay on long past dinner. I know my husband.

After I dressed and quickly gave myself the once-over in front of the floor-length mirror, I quickly brushed my thick hair, pulled it into a French knot and finished setting the dinner table with red candles to give a romantic, intimate setting. Brice still hadn't arrived home yet and the steaks needed a few more minutes to cook, so I sat on our black leather sofa to wait and think.

I truly hated to lie to my husband, but sometimes it was necessary to keep the peace. Mother always told me that a man doesn't have to know everything. Keep some secrets. Today I went to check out a help-wanted ad I had seen in the classified section of the *Atlanta Journal-Constitution*.

I loved to dance, and a boys-and-girls club near Midtown was looking for dance instructors to teach modern dance in an after-school program they offered. The pay wasn't that great, but at least it involved dancing. I had to start somewhere. Unfortunately I was too late, because the position had already been filled.

It's probably for the best. Brice doesn't want me to work anyway, which is fine with me. I'm happy being a traditional wife. As long as I can pamper myself with manicures, pedicures, and salon appointments every other week, I'm fine.

We have been in Atlanta for a little over three months now. It's different, in a good way, living in Atlanta, because I have never lived in the South before. I am originally from Philadelphia, although I've traveled all over the world with my family. My mother is back in

Philly and my older brother, Miles, lives out in California with his second wife, Vanessa, and new daughter, Taylor.

Hotlanta, however, is home for Brice. When he had gotten an honorable discharge from the marines, he was excited about being near his aging parents, Vivica and Robert, and they were pleased to have him nearby again. I looked forward to the opportunity to get to know them better, especially his mother, Vivica. Whenever we talked, she was always so nice to me. She welcomed me into the fold with open arms and a big smile.

Yeah, Brice is definitely in his element. If things go as planned, he'll start a small security-consulting business soon. Yes, things are going well for us. We can't complain; I can't complain. Brice is good to me. Most of the time. I pretty much receive anything I ask for as long as I please him.

It didn't take long to discover that to make Brice happy I had to do what he wanted me to do: stroke his ego, prepare him good meals and act like a whore in bed. In return I received a man who loved me, protected me, made me feel like a woman and gave me a good, secure life. I think that's an even trade. So no, I can't complain most of the time.

The only glitch in moving to Atlanta is this Christian person. Why is there always a glitch? I never really heard the entire story from start to finish. Brice is so secretive about it, and I don't push him for info. But from what I could piece together, Brice and Christian were like brothers years ago until Brice got a messy divorce from Mia, and Christian ended up marrying Mia. What kind of woman marries her ex-husband's best friend? That's too close to being incestuous. Anyway, there was a lot of in-between that I missed.

And now Brice wants Christian—and Mia—back in his life, our lives. I'm not too thrilled about that, but Brice usually gets what Brice wants. I know he misses Christian because he's always talking about the good old days, but Mia comes with Christian. You can't get one without the other. Mia and Christian are a package deal.

Mia. I don't know how I feel about her. Jealous, perhaps. I've seen photos of Mia and she's a beautiful woman. I'm keeping it real. She is. I could never understand why Brice had never destroyed his pictures of her; after all, they're divorced. Why hold on to those memories? But it doesn't matter; I have him now. He's in my bed every night.

I remember once when we had just started dating, back in Germany, I spent the night for the first time with Brice. In the early-morning hours, after we had made love twice and fallen fast asleep, a sleepy Brice reached out for me, pulled me close and called me Mia. It upset me, but I never mentioned it to him. It was only later that I discovered, much to my dismay, that Mia is his ex-wife. No, I am definitely not looking forward to this little reunion.

I believe that you can keep going long after you can't.
—Author Unknown

As Christian hoisted Lyric up onto his shoulder and reached for my hand, we walked out of Zoo Atlanta tired but happy. Lyric was exhausted as well. She had been excited about seeing the new panda bears. She had pointed at the various animals, played, and eaten enough popcorn and ice cream for two. I knew she would sleep peacefully throughout the night. Lyric looked so cute in her little blue-and-white capri pant set with her hair in two long braids.

When I look at her, I see a miniature, female version of Christian. The two of them together always make my heart feel warm and bubbly inside. It still amazes me that Christian and I produced such a beautiful, adorable child. We made the short trek up the hill to our car in comfortable silence. Since the zoo was closing, the parking lot was quickly emptying, with families heading home on this beautiful spring day.

I studied Christian out the corner of my eye. I love him so much that it's scary. After Brice, I never imagined I could love again or give myself to a man so completely. Christian changed all that for me. He is the sort of man that women dream of . . . From his ripped stomach, toned from hours of boxing, running and weight lifting, to his goatee and sexy eyes, I adore him. He is such a strong, patient and forgiving man. Christian needs those traits to deal with me and, unfortunately, I realize that.

The last few weeks have been difficult for both of us, to say the least. I can't believe that Christian would ask me *again* to meet with

Brice. When he had brought it up weeks earlier, I thought he fully understood my feelings. Since he evidently hadn't, I made life hell for him.

I gave one-word answers to his questions, I wouldn't iniate a conversation with him and I wouldn't let him touch me in bed. I didn't say no, but I would just lie there like a stone. During his kisses on the neck and light caresses, I would just lie there with my legs closed. He got the hint. Christian, throughout it all, remained patient and understanding with me. Sometimes, like now, I feel as if I don't deserve him in my life.

I had almost made my decision about meeting Brice. After a strained few days with Christian and after talking it over with Mama, I felt I was ready to make a final decision. Maybe they were all right and I was wrong. Maybe it was time to put final closure on the past once and for all. Closure is something I never reached with Brice. After leaving him, I never set eyes on Brice again. I didn't want anything from him. I just needed peace of mind. Mama and my attorney handled Brice and our divorce. I signed the documents, relished my freedom and tried to get my life back on track. Maybe I should have talked with Brice and asked him why before moving on with my life. At the time I didn't trust myself with him. He had a way of getting me to do things I didn't want to do. I think it's called manipulation.

If Christian and I met with Brice—for what purpose I don't know—maybe the nightmares would stop. Who knows? And as Mama pointed out, Christian lost someone who was like a brother to him, so he has been grieving as well.

We made it to the car and Christian managed to get Lyric settled in her booster seat without waking her. We were ready to go home.

"You haven't said two words since we left the zoo. I thought you enjoyed yourself today." Christian looked at me as he held the door open for me to get in.

"I'm fine, baby. I just have a lot on my mind. Lyric really enjoyed herself today. She'll definitely sleep through the night."

By now Christian had gotten in on the driver's side and was checking the rearview mirror and getting ready to back out. I reached over to gently touch his shoulder. "Boo, wait for a minute. We need to talk," I said seriously. "I know the last few weeks haven't been easy for you, because I've acted like the bitch from hell. I apologize. I'm selfish and I'm working on that, but I've been thinking, and—"

Christian interrupted me with, "You don't have to—"

"No, wait, let me finish. Let's meet with Brice and his wife and see what he has to say. I'm sure it will be the usual BS, but I know you have missed him all these years and want to see him. I just want you to know that I'm doing this for you, Boo."

With that, Christian leaned over, and took my face between his hands so that he was looking directly into my eyes.

"Are you sure?"

"Yes, I'm scared, but sure," I answered with a slight tremble to my voice.

"Good, that's my girl. Don't worry; I'll be right there by your side. I got your back, baby," he said as he gave me a serious kiss that I felt down to my toes.

Christian

The storm has passed for now! Mia always keeps me guessing. We've been married for almost four years and she still keeps me on my toes. I had talked with Mia's mom, who treats me like a son, about this situation, and I still didn't know what decision Mia would reach. Either way, I wasn't going to force the meeting on her. I was pleasantly surprised with her announcement when we were leaving Zoo Atlanta.

What I didn't tell Mia was that Brice and I had met a week ago for drinks at MVP's off of Memorial Drive. I knew her feelings for him and figured what she didn't know couldn't hurt her.

I arrived first at MVP's and was sitting at the bar nursing a cold beer when Brice, who was running a few minutes late, made an appearance. I knew the moment he walked through the door, because I noticed a few women looking in his direction, checking him out from head to toe. Once Brice spotted me sitting at the crowded bar, he strolled confidently in my direction. Just as he entered my space, I set my beer on the countertop and stood to greet him. We were face-to-face, eye-to-eye for the first time in years. Brice stared, I looked back, and then we both broke into huge smiles.

"Christian, man, it's good to see you. It's been a long time. How've you been?" he asked, his strong handshake turning into an emotional embrace.

"I can't complain. Life is good; I'm happy."

"Yeah, you look good; you look well taken care of," Brice said as he stared at me.

"Same to you, man."

Still standing, we stood man-to-man for a few more minutes with those grins on our faces.

"Man, this is harder than I thought it would be. It's good to see you. I mean that, and I have so much explaining to do." We took a seat at the bar.

"Well, I have all the time you need. You know how we used to close the bar out," I reminded him with a genuine smile. The bartender came over, we paused in conversation, and Brice ordered a beer as well.

"Christian, first of all, I'm sorry. Forgive me. I had problems back then that I've tried hard to resolve."

That was how our meeting began. It was a bit awkward for the first few minutes, but after we sat down and actually started talking, things felt natural. I felt like I had been reunited with a long-lost relative. We didn't talk too long about any deep issues; we kept everything casual, reminiscing about the good old days.

Brice hadn't changed much since our military years together. If anything, he was more buff and toned and as arrogant as ever. Brice looked happy and at peace with himself. He showed me a photo of his new wife, Kree, and, as expected, she was beautiful, with long, thick, shoulder-length hair, high cheekbones and deep, penetrating eyes. There was a familiarity about her. Kree was definitely a looker. He always did know how to pick women.

I showed him a recent photo of Mia and Lyric, the one with them dressed all in white, and he got a distant look in his eyes that soon passed as our conversation changed to catching up on old friends and acquaintances. By now we had moved our conversation and drinks to a table near the wall.

The conversation was lively, the drinks ever flowing, and the evening passed quickly. Before I knew it, we were shaking hands and saying good night. Brice gave me his address and phone number again and we made plans to meet soon.

Brice

As I made my way home from MVP's about a week ago, my ringing cell phone pulled me out of my reverie.

"Yeah?"

"Baby, are you on your way home?" Kree asked in a slightly annoying, babylike voice. "I miss you."

"I know you didn't call to check up on me," I said, irritated.

"Brice, don't start getting mad. I wanted to know how the meeting went."

"Can you at least wait until I walk through the door?" Lately Kree has been getting on my last nerve. She's always asking me these damn questions about Mia. How did she look, what were the details of the breakup, how was Mia in bed? It was like she was trying to compete!

"Well, I'm waiting up for you . . . in bed. I've got a surprise for you."

"Okay, I'll see you in ten minutes," I said in a distracted voice before hanging up.

My thoughts immediately went back to Mia. When Christian showed me that photo of her, I had to catch my breath. She was breathtaking; five years had only enhanced her beauty. It took me a few moments, which Christian missed, to compose myself as I conjured up images of him screwing her. Mia wasn't a virgin when I married her, but she hadn't been with too many men, so I taught her quite a few things in the bedroom.

I missed that about her; she totally gave her body to me with no inhibitions. Her pussy craved my dick. I couldn't picture her—didn't want to picture her—screwing some other brotha. Especially if that other brotha was Christian.

Within minutes I was parking my white Volvo and walking up the flight of steps to my condo we were leasing. When I inserted my key and opened the front door, I noticed a glow illuminating the hallway. I didn't even investigate; I just sat down on the sofa and turned on the TV out of habit, lost in my own thoughts and images of the past.

Kree interrupted my thoughts. "Brice, what's taking you so long? Come on back!"

I got up. As I walked slowly down the hallway, my mind was still a million miles away.

"Baby?"

When I entered our bedroom and looked up, Kree was lying on our bed spread-eagled on a canopy of roses with candles, tons of candles, every shape and shade of red you could imagine, lit throughout the room. There wasn't a space void of candles. Kree had this look of "come fuck me" on her face, and for once in our marriage, I wasn't interested.

"Kree, I'm tired, baby. Thanks for all the trouble you went through, but you're going to have to take a rain check." I sat on the edge of our king-size bed and began to undress. I slowly pulled off my shoes and trousers, and started to unbutton my shirt with my back to her. However, I could feel her intense glare.

"Give me a minute and I'll help you blow out all the candles," I offered without moving an inch.

Kree came up behind me and wrapped her slender arms around my neck, her breasts caressing my back. Kree was blessed in that department. She knew that was my weakness.

"Kree, stop, I'm tired," I said forcefully as I unwrapped her arms from around my neck.

Kree was taken aback, but only for a few moments before she wrapped her arms around my neck once again and whispered, "Oh, you go and see your old friend—who, by the way, is married to your ex-wife—and suddenly now you don't want me?"

"It's not like that, Kree; I'm just tired. I'll give you some in the morning. You can sit up and bitch and moan, but I'm going to bed."

I finished undressing down to my underwear and pulled back the navy satin sheet.

Kree finally made it back to bed after blowing out the candles. She wasn't trying to hide her obvious annoyance. She slid her body over against mine; there wasn't an inch of space left between us. I could feel her silky nakedness. Normally it would have had me hard as a brick, but tonight it irritated the hell out of me.

"Baby, how did it go?"

"Fine."

"Are we meeting Christian's family?"

"I don't know yet."

"Why not, baby?"

"What is this, twenty damn questions? Get some sleep, Kree; I'll talk to you in the morning," I said with anger in my voice.

Kree knew when to shut the fuck up, but she still insisted on invading my space.

Staring into space, I lay there with my back to her as she continued to wrap her long legs around my waist. Finally I could take no more.

I turned around, grabbed her and straddled her before she knew what hit her.

"You want some dick, Kree? Is that what you want? Okay, I'm going to give you some." I began to kiss her roughly on her lips.

Kree instantly started protesting. So I grabbed her by the hair and pushed her back down.

"Come on, now, open your legs wide for Daddy. I'm going to give you what you want."

Kree was kicking and screaming, trying her best to get me off her as my fingers found her spot while my teeth bit her neck. I admit I was relentless. The more she fought me, the more excited I became.

"Leave me alone, Brice. Stop! You bastard."

I had her pinned down on the bed with my full weight on her. One hand held her arms above her head as I stroked and touched her wherever I pleased.

"Do you like that? Yeah, you like that. I know you do. Come on, come on now, open wider, baby."

I pushed her legs open even farther with my knees and kept right on stroking. When she started to cry, I flipped her over on her stomach so I wouldn't have to see her face, held her head down with my hand and entered her from behind in a savage fury. I pumped and pumped in and out until I was exhausted. Then I pulled out, released her slowly, rolled over and was out a few minutes after my head hit the pillow.

Kree

I believe that we are responsible for what we do, no matter how we feel.   —Author Unknown

I lovingly admired, rearranged and smelled the bouquet of red roses that had arrived earlier that morning courtesy of the local florist's shop. The attached note, from Brice, simply read: *I was wrong; please forgive me!* After what happened a week earlier, I had been giving Brice the cold shoulder. All I had wanted that night was to make love to my husband and share in celebrating his reunion with Christian. I really wasn't mad any longer, but I was curious to see how far he would go to romance me and place himself back in my good graces. The ring of the phone brought me out of my daydreaming.

"Hello?"

"Hey, baby. Did you receive your surprise yet? I know how much you love roses," Brice said in his humblest voice.

"Yeah, they arrived about an hour ago," I answered, uninterested.

"Well . . ."

"Well, what?"

"Do you like them? You know, Kree, you aren't making this easy," Brice said in an exasperated manner. "I've been trying for over a week to apologize for that night. I don't know what else to say or do. I've admitted I had a lot on my mind, what with the business plans, the loan, our move . . . There is just a lot going on, baby."

"I know that, and believe me, I'm on your side. I love you, baby. I'd do anything for you."

"Well, you aren't acting like you love me. You could have fooled me."

"Brice, you shouldn't have treated me like some whore from the street. Sometimes I see this side of you that I don't like and it scares me."

"Again, I'm sorry. I don't know what else to say. I love you, baby, and it won't happen again. Do you forgive me? Come on, say you forgive me."

After a long pause, I finally gave in. "Yes, Brice, you are still my man . . . and I forgive you."

After hanging up the phone with instructions from Brice to have his dinner ready, I wondered if I should have made him suffer for another few days. I knew my husband, and he couldn't go too long without sex. Since I hadn't let him touch me since that night, I knew he was majorly horny.

As I prepared a chicken-and-shrimp stir-fry, fixed a light Caesar salad, and took out some French bread to toast, I thought about what I had told Brice earlier. I meant every word. I loved him so much and would do almost anything for him. Brice was my everything.

That first night I saw him, something inside of me just opened up and I knew he was the one. I know that sounds super corny, but I did—I knew he was the one. We talked all night about everything and nothing at all. I felt like I had known him all my life. The age difference meant nothing; it was just a number. However, sometimes I see a hint of his bad temper that he tries hard to hide. He's possessive and somewhat controlling, but he's a strong man, and I know that he loves me.

Later that evening, much to my surprise, Brice arrived home with yet another present. I was shocked. I thought the roses were the finale.

He took off his jacket, tossed it on the love seat, and gently pulled me onto his lap with a kiss. I asked, "What's this?" as I shook the box wrapped in beautiful red-and-gold gift paper with a big red bow.

With a mischievous grin, he said, "Open it. Here, let me help you."

"No, I can do it myself," I said, playfully slapping his hands away.

I purposely took my time opening the package and repositioned myself on his lap. I could feel his hardness pressing against me. Brice is well-endowed and has been truly blessed in that department. And the man knows how to use his equipment.

Finally, I opened the package and pulled out a sexy, see-through, flaming-red negligee with matching silk panties, which were just as skimpy. The attached tag read, *Frederick's of Hollywood*.

"Try it on. Model for me," Brice said in a deep, sexy tone with a sultry look in his eyes.

Yeah, he wanted some. I got up to go into the bedroom.

"No, try it on in here." He pulled me back between his open legs, gently rubbing and slapping my butt through the fabric of my dress.

I pulled away and debated whether I should give him his wish or not.

"Undress for your man, baby. Let me see my stuff," he whispered.

Slowly and seductively, I unfastened the tiny buttons down the front of my full-skirted black dress. Brice's eyes never left me.

"That's right, take your time. Give me a show."

I stepped out of my dress, lightly licked my lips and stood in front of Brice in my lacy black bra-and-panty set, my legs slightly parted.

"Go on; take it off. Take it all off. Show me my stuff."

Brice loves for me to play this strip-tease game with him. He says it turned him on big-time to reveal my body to him, little by little.

After unclipping the front hook, I slid my right bra strap off my shoulder, then my left bra strap. I held my bra in place with my hands. Just as I dropped them, I turned my back to Brice. Bending down, with one swift movement I was out of my thong. I turned back around to see Brice's reaction. He didn't disappoint. He always made me feel like a woman. The lust in his eyes, the way his gaze traveled over my body from head to toe, I knew I was desired. Very desired.

Brice approached me and had my nipple in his mouth before I could object. A small moan escaped my lips when I felt his finger inside me.

It took a lot, but I pushed him back. "Remember, I'm modeling for you."

"Come here, Kree, I want some pussy." He palmed my butt cheeks and rubbed. With his free hand, he unzipped his pants.

"Poor baby."

"Oh, poor baby, my ass. You know you want to ride this." He held his organ in his hand and stroked up and down.

I pushed him back again and slipped into the red negligee. It was the perfect fit, what little there was, and it complemented my body. It showed everything I had to offer. By now Brice was looking like he was going to explode.

"Kree, are you going to tease me all night?"

"I'd never do that, baby," I purred in a naughty voice. "I'm going to give you some just like you like it."

"Come here, baby." He reached for me again.

Again, I pulled back just in time.

"You didn't want me the other night, remember? So you've got to prove you want me now."

"Believe me, I want you, baby. Look, my jimmy wants you so bad that he's saluting you." He pulled me onto the sofa and began to suckle and caress my breasts again, moving his hand up and down between my thighs.

"No, show me, Brice."

Brice knew what I was talking about. He rarely went down on me, but it turned me on so much when he did that I thought I was losing my mind. He had me sucking his dick all the time, though. When we first married, Brice made me watch these porno movies so that I could get the technique down. And Brice is huge. Sometimes he wouldn't give me any unless I did that for him. Now the tables were turned.

Brice realized I was serious. When he walked away into the kitchen, I wasn't sure what he was up to. He quickly returned with one of our dining room chairs and placed me gently in it as he continued to caress me. Brice proceeded to pull me to the edge of the seat, pulled my negligee up to my waist and grabbed my ankles, placing them on the chair rests.

My stuff was literally in his face. He got on his knees and opened my legs even wider, if that was possible. He was definitely up close and personal. As he lowered his mouth and began to grant my request, I threw my head back in ecstasy.

Mia

"Mommy, Mommy, look," Lyric shouted as she ran back and forth on her short, stubby legs from Mama to me. We were at Northlake Mall, off Lavista Road, relaxing on a bench after an exhausting shopping spree. Mama, Lyric, and myself were now indulging in Baskin-Robbins ice cream. It was butter pecan for me, strawberry for Lyric, and rocky road for Mama. It had been a full day helping Mama shop for a Carnival cruise she was going on in a few weeks. Her first one.

She's come a long way. Years earlier she would have never even thought about going on a senior citizens' cruise to the Bahamas. A few years ago a liquor bottle was her best friend and companion. However, that's all in the past. Mama has been sober for almost five years and still attends AA meetings regularly. It hasn't been an easy road, not by a long shot. But she's doing just fine. Now her life is full of good friends, bingo, church and her only granddaughter.

Lyric was getting more ice cream on Mama than in her own little mouth.

"The other day when Christian picked up Lyric, he told me that y'all are going to meet with that fool," Mama said as she smiled at Lyric, who was now back on the floor walking back and forth.

"Yes, Mama, we haven't set a time or place yet, but we are meeting with him and his new wife. I think her name is Kree. It'll make Christian happy, and that's what's important to me. Even though he won't admit it, I know he has missed having Brice in his life. After everything that's happened, Christian lost the most—his adopted family."

"I think you're doing the right thing for your husband and even yourself. You need this closure. You look Brice straight in the eyes and you let him know that he didn't destroy your spirit. You be careful, though, baby. I still don't trust that man as far as I can throw him. Any man who would hit a woman . . . Lord have mercy. After all that mess he put you through . . ."

"I know; I will. Like I said, I'm doing this for Christian. If I had my way, I'd never set eyes on the man again."

"Why now, though, why after almost five years? That's what I can't figure out. It doesn't make sense," Mama wondered.

"I know; I've thought about that too. But he's been overseas most of this time, and it couldn't possibly be because his conscience is bothering him." Lyric jumped back into my lap, hugged me, and gave me a sticky kiss on the nose.

"His wife, poor thing, what does she think about this li'l meeting?"

"Honestly, I don't know, Mama, and I really don't care," I huffed with too much attitude, which caused Mama to give me one of her looks. One of her "do you know who you're talking to?" looks.

As she gazed into space she said, "I don't ever want to see you in that state of mind again. During that period, you were in such emotional despair. A parent can't stand seeing her child in pain. That man totally broke my baby's spirit . . ."

"Let's talk about something else. I'm sick of hearing about Brice. We're giving him too much importance, too much power," I said in a shaky voice.

Mama looked at me out of the corner of her eyes. "Okay, baby. Be careful. Just be careful. I don't want to see you hurt again. You've got a good man in Christian. Men like Christian don't come around every day."

Mama and I, along with Lyric in her Mickey Mouse stroller, went to a few more stores and eventually called it a day around four o'clock.

On the drive home I thought about what Mama had said. I was a sad, pitiful case during my divorce to Brice. My heart was split wide-open. Most days, I couldn't even get out of bed. I just wanted to sleep. I felt like my life was over. I had my good and bad days, but Mama was there through it all. I promised myself I'd never give a man that much power in my life again—as much as I love Christian, not even him. No, I don't want to see myself in that state again.

"Is that cool with you, baby? Let me know if it's not, because we can change the time," I asked Mia for probably the third time that day.

"Christian, like I told you before, that's fine with me. I'll double-check and make sure Mama can babysit Lyric," Mia assured me as she sexily sashayed into the kitchen to finish up the dinner dishes. I admired her from the kitchen table. It was another lazy Sunday afternoon and tomorrow was business as usual, back to the work routine. Mia's lucky; she has a few more months and then she'll be out for summer break. Schoolteachers have it made in that area. After a school year with some of those kids, they need a break. Mia has tons of stories to tell about some of their badasses.

We had finally come up with a date, two weeks from Saturday, to meet with Brice and Kree. To make it convenient for Mia, we decided to have a light meal at our house and take it from there. Surprisingly, Mia is taking everything in stride. She was truly amazing. I know she's doing all this for me. I realize I'm probably being selfish, but I miss our true friendship, the ties of brotherhood that Brice and I had once shared. I was hoping, on some level, that we could move forward and recapture that. Yes, I'm being selfish.

As I heard Mia humming away in the kitchen, clinking dishes now and then, I thought back to how we got together. After Mia's breakup with Brice, I was as emotionally devastated as she was. Mia had lost a husband, but after admitting to Brice that I was in love with Mia, I had lost a lifelong best friend. In giving up our friendship, I also gave up any ties to Brice's family. That was entirely my choice.

In the beginning, his moms, Vivica, was constantly calling to see how I was doing. She'd chitchat about whatever was going on in her life. When I wasn't very receptive, her calls eventually dwindled down to one or two a month and then to nonexistent. Afterward, I was pretty much alone in life. That suited me fine, because most of my life had been spent alone—emotionally anyway.

My brother, Randy, was killed as a teenager. He never lived to see eighteen. My moms had died when I was in high school and I never knew my pops. Since I had never formed too many attachments or friendships, I was literally all alone. Looking back, if I had to do it all over again, I'd still make the same decision. I had to choose and I chose Mia.

After Mia and Brice's breakup, she left North Carolina and returned home to Georgia and to her moms. I soon got into the routine of calling her once a week, usually on Sundays, just to check up on her. Mia was in so much pain. Most of the time she was just lying around or in bed. She didn't go anywhere, didn't see anyone, never left the house except for work. I used to tell her that she made the start of my work-week bearable because I could focus on making it through the week so that I could talk to her on Sunday. Mia just laughed at that, which was something she didn't do a lot of, and told me I was so silly. Her laughter was music to my ears.

Eventually the phone calls turned into short weekend visits and, in between, there were "just because" cards, e-mails and letters mailed to each other. My visits were always platonic, because even though Mia was divorced by then, it seemed that an invisible Brice was always with us. An ever-seeing force. Mia never brought up his name or mentioned anything about her life with him, but he was always there with us. An unseen presence.

I felt guilty that I had fallen in love with her. Now, I know that we can't help whom we love. The heart can't lie. The heart won't lie. Every time I felt a gush of love for Mia, I felt like I betrayed Brice. Sure, he was possessive, hot-tempered, jealous and always beating on her when they were married. Mia had made the right decision by leaving him, yet I felt like I was being disloyal.

So . . . I denied my feelings and kept everything platonic. I wasn't dating anyone, and it was hard being close to Mia without being able to act on my feelings, but at least she was in my presence and in my life. That brought me great joy. A hug from her, a kiss on the cheek, her laughter—it brought me joy.

Mia was slowly returning to her old self, the one I fell in love with. Usually a flirt, she kept her emotional distance from me as well. Yet occasionally I'd see glimpses of her previous spirit. What finally changed our entire relationship was a wedding and a snowstorm in Virginia. To this day, that state has a soft spot in my heart.

Mia asked me to ride with her to her cousin Linda's wedding in Baltimore one cold weekend. I agreed, Mia met me in North Carolina and off we drove on our merry way. The wedding was beautiful as far as weddings go, and Linda made a gorgeous bride. According to Mia, she had finally snagged that pilot she had her eyes on all those years. I remembered meeting Linda years back. She was cool people.

Mia was simply stunning in a black dress that showed off her curves. During the ceremony, now and then, Mia would glance over at me sitting to her right. I loved it when she'd lean over and touch the back of my neck to whisper something in my ear. Just her touch was magical. I could feel a change taking place. Barriers were falling down, chip by chip. Throughout the ceremony, Mia would sneak a peek at me when she thought I wasn't looking. A few times our eyes met and she gave her dazzling smile, just for me. By the end of the ceremony we were holding hands with our fingers firmly entwined. It felt right for the first time.

After an elaborate reception with a live band and sit-down dinner, we changed into jeans at Linda's apartment and decided to drive back home through the night and early-morning hours. Mia and I didn't count on a snowstorm. Unfortunately, we hadn't paid much attention to weather reports that evening. Mia and I had just about made it to the Virginia border when visibility became almost nil and, to top that off, we were both tired from the day's events.

When it looked like it was going to be too dangerous to continue, we stopped at motel after hotel looking for a vacancy. However, everyone else on the road had had the same idea. There weren't any vacancies anywhere.

Finally, luck was on our side, and we secured the last room at a Holiday Inn spin-off. Since there was only one room available, we had to share. It was a decent room with two full-size beds. At least we were warm and had a roof over our heads. The news reported that the storm was far-reaching and had surprised and stranded a lot of motorists.

Once Mia and I were settled we took our individual showers and got ready to retire for the night. I noticed Mia hadn't said too much since our arrival, but I assumed she was just tired. Now and again I caught her staring at me. Earlier, when I had stepped out of the hot shower, I realized I had forgotten to bring my T-shirt into the bathroom. So I wrapped one of the white hotel towels around my waist. It was no big deal; Mia was a grown woman and had seen a man's chest before. However, when I walked out to retrieve my shirt out of my black travel bag, Mia couldn't answer a simple question. She couldn't even look at me and kept her head down.

Later, when she was taking her shower, I reclined back on one of the beds, watched TV, and imagined Mia showering, lathering sudsy soap over her body, and daydreamed about being with her. Mia finished up, came out dressed in a long T-shirt thingy, smiled at me, said good night and hopped into the full-size bed next to mine.

I fell asleep with visions of her ample breasts, which I had seen through her thin T-shirt. Later that night I awoke to someone calling out my name, softly at first and then more urgently. I rubbed sleep from my eyes and tried to focus in the darkness. It was pitch-black in the room and I couldn't see a thing. When I finally focused, Mia was standing above my bed without a stitch of clothing on. She was looking down at me. I shook my head and focused because I thought I was imagining things or having an erotic dream.

When Mia called out my name again, I didn't say a word. I pulled the covers back and she got in and sought my mouth. It was a sweet kiss as our tongues met and explored the mystery of each other. We had waited too long for this moment. The kiss went on for a few minutes until Mia pulled away.

"Christian, show me all the love I feel from you," she cooed as my lips touched her neck, making her shiver.

My hands began an exploration of her body, inch by precious inch. I asked, "Are you sure? There's no turning back once we do this."

She nodded her head and smiled. "I've never been surer of anything in my life."

It was on, to put it mildly! We loved each other like two people starving for a simple touch. I felt, kneaded, rubbed, caressed and tasted her entire body from head to toe. When Mia slowly eased her sweetness onto my throbbing manhood, we meshed as one, and she started our ride so slowly, so sensually, that I thought I had died and gone to heaven. We were like a rocket ship. As the acceleration picked up, with me guiding her hips and rising to meet her with my own, her pace increased. Her back was arched, head thrown back, eyes glazed over, breasts bouncing, and we continued our dance. I was hard as a steel pipe, almost exploding, pulling back, squeezing, moving in and out. I was reaching for her nipples, moaning, Mia sucked my fingers one by one into her warm mouth.

Frantic breathing, couldn't catch my breath. Calling out her name over and over, praising her loveliness, adoring her body, worshiping her power, loving her, giving all I had to give . . . Then one last thrust . . . I remember rolling over on top of her as she instinctively wrapped her legs around my back, and then flying to the top of the rocket ship with her name on my lips, my eyes rolling back in my head. *Miaaaaaaaaaa.*

Mia and I stayed up the rest of the night talking, really talking. Wrapped in each other's arms, for the first time we shared our true feelings for each other, and Brice's presence wasn't in the room with us. We felt as one, and before we left for home we were one again. This time, it was slow and gentle. Eye-to-eye. Spiritual.

After that, Mia consumed my life every waking hour, and, shortly afterward, we recited our wedding vows to each other in an intimate ceremony. We wrote our own vows to each other, promising to faithfully love, forever cherish and always honor each other, through good and bad times, to be there for each other through sickness and health, until the day we die. And in over three and a half years, I haven't regretted a second of making those vows. Not a second.

"Christian, man, thank you for giving me this opportunity to redeem myself. Believe it or not, I do have a conscience," I said to Christian, who had called me on my cell phone to confirm our get-together next Saturday evening at eight.

"Not a problem; I think we all need to resolve some unfinished issues," Christian declared with much sincerity in his voice. "Brice, I hope this is all for the best. For everyone concerned. Do me a favor—if it looks like the evening isn't going well, leave. I'm not going to force this on Mia."

"It's done, man. I've still got your back, regardless of the differences we've faced these last few years."

"Cool, Brice. You're still my dog."

"Should we bring anything?"

"Just yourselves. We've got it covered like a blanket. Man, I hope this isn't a mistake."

"It's not; trust me."

Christian and I talked awhile longer about Moms and my pops. Pops's health had deteriorated little by little over the last five years. His doctor diagnosed him with the initial stages of Alzheimer's. It's truly sad to see a man who was once so strong, vibrant and unstoppable reduced to the shell of a person I see each time Kree and I stop by to visit. Year by year, he's losing his memory and his ability to take care of himself. Moms is dealing with it, though, but of course she would—that's Moms. Regardless of everything Pops has put her through, she loves him dearly. I truly believe that, because Pops has taken Moms through some heavy shit.

I'm relieved to be back in the area, because I can take some of the daily stress off of her. I don't want Moms to become a prisoner in her own home. She had been that when I was a child. Back then, Pops didn't play. His word was the law in our household. And you best believe he ruled with an iron fist. Unfortunately, Moms was usually on the receiving end.

Christian and I finally said our good-byes and I hung up as tons of memories flooded me. I thought back to the relationship he and I had shared in the past. The man was once like a blood brother to me. We were close, to say the least. At school, they used to call us the Two Musketeers.

Hell, Christian and I grew up together. We even got our first taste of some ass from the same hoochie, all within the same week. What was her name . . . ? I can't even remember now. She'd dropped her drawers for practically every male at the school. Christian and I have been through so much together—both good and bad. I only hope we can recapture what we once shared—a true friendship. I miss that. I didn't realize how much until recently.

The ringing of my cell phone brought me out of my reverie and back to reality. I slowly drove down Auburn Avenue, watching my African American brothers and sisters as they tended to their daily lives. That's what I love about Atlanta; it's the mecca of black America. There is black history everywhere. If you can't make it here, then you can't make it anywhere.

"Hello?"

"Mr. Matthew?"

"Yes, this is he," I answered, trying to place the voice on the other end of the line. It was a young-sounding male who sounded familiar.

"Mr. Matthew, this is Mr. Petty, over at National Bank. I wanted to be the first to congratulate you. Your loan has been approved."

I didn't hear his next comments because I was too busy thinking about my next steps. How long would it take me to be up and operational? How many employees would I need to hire?

"Mr. Matthew? Are you still there?"

"Yes, my cell went out of range for a few seconds. I'm here. Please go on."

"Well, all we need now is your signature on the dotted line. What is a convenient time for you to come in?"

"I can be there first thing in the morning." I tried to contain my growing excitement. "How about ten o'clock?"

"Ten o'clock it is. We'll see you then. Again, congratulations and welcome to the National Bank family."

"Thank you." I hung up, still in awe.

As I stopped at the traffic light, I couldn't believe how great my day had been going. Life was definitely looking up. First the news from Christian; then the loan went through, and I even had a few possible locations for my office space. I'd been scouting out prime locations. Three looked promising, and the overhead wouldn't be too steep.

The light changed from red to green and I slowly pulled off and picked up my cell to call home. The phone rang three times and Kree picked up.

"Hello?"

"Hey, baby. I've got great news!" I shouted right off the bat.

"You got the loan?" Kree asked with mounting excitement in her tone.

"Yeah, the loan officer just called. After I sign the papers, it's a done deal, baby. After ten o'clock tomorrow morning, I'll be an entrepreneur."

"I'm so proud of you, baby. I knew you could do it. Your proposal was so well written, and there's a definite need for your services." Kree spoke with obvious pride in her voice.

"Thanks, baby. Listen, get dressed in that sexy red dress I love to see you in, and I'm taking you out to Justin's for a celebratory dinner. I'll be there in fifteen."

Kree had been talking about going to Justin's for two months. Up until now we couldn't afford to splurge. But tonight we were going to live it up and celebrate the start of a new venture.

Once I arrived home, I showered and dressed in record time. I dressed from head to toe in black, looking good and feeling fine.

Kree was stunning in her sexy red dress with the plunging neckline. I admired her for a few seconds. Stunning. She adorned it with a pair of slinky, strap-on red shoes and a simple pair of diamond-stud earrings that I'd given her for her birthday last year. Kree was beautiful, breathtaking. She has a way of looking at me, batting her long eyelashes, pouting her full lips a certain way, that made me weak at the knees. She knows how to turn me on, and I know how to turn her out.

I splashed on a little of my favorite cologne, checked out my hair one last time and headed out the door hand in hand with my lady.

On the ride over, Kree talked nonstop about what a great businessman I would make, how successful I was going to be and how proud she was of me. I must admit, Kree has always been supportive of my endeavors. She's a good wife and loves to please and take care of her man. She's mature for her age. I guess that comes from traveling abroad and being exposed to other cultures at such an early age. Sometimes I forget she's only twenty-five.

After we left our car with the valet to be parked, Kree and I made our way to the entrance of Justin's. The wait for a table wasn't as long as I expected, but there was a huge after-hours crowd at the bar laughing and having a good time. The atmosphere was trendy, and the crowd consisted mostly of black professionals out for an enjoyable evening. There were many attractive black women in the place. It was amazing how many of them tried to make eye contact with me even with Kree on my arm.

After a twenty-minute wait, Kree and I were seated at an intimate corner table. She kept smiling at me, showing me her pearly whites. I leaned over, cupped her face and gave her a kiss that lasted for a few seconds.

She leaned over to wipe the red lipstick off of me. "What was that for?"

"Oh, I can't kiss my wife now?" I asked in mock indignation.

"Anytime, anywhere, anyplace. You aren't usually so affectionate in public, that's all."

"Well, you look so beautiful and sexy tonight that I can't keep my hands off of you. Later, I can't wait to show you how beautiful you are."

Kree blushed and looked at me with love and devotion reflected in her eyes. We hadn't been seated long when our waiter came over and took our dinner and drink orders. I chose for both of us.

We sat and sipped our white wine in a comfortable silence. I had purchased an entire bottle to start off our celebration. At one point she entwined her hand with mine. A warm, radiant feeling engulfed me. So many men searched high and low to find a woman who loved them unconditionally. I found that in Kree.

I know for a fact that she'd do almost anything, shy of murder, to keep me happy and satisfied. Sometimes I ask her to do things in bed that she doesn't really want to do. Under different circumstances, she probably wouldn't do them, but Kree loves me and lives to please me. Lately, I've had all these fantasies that I wanted to act out. I admit, sex is very important to me.

"Listen, baby, in all the excitement, I forgot to tell you I talked to Christian today."

"And . . . ?"

"Well, we are meeting with them next Saturday at eight P.M."

Kree didn't say anything at first. She looked away so I couldn't see the expression on her face.

"Kree?"

"What, Brice?" she asked, slightly annoyed.

"Is that cool?"

"Do I have a choice? This is what you want, right? It's all you've talked about since we moved here."

"Baby, you have a choice. I don't know why you'd think that," I said a bit perturbed.

"Probably because you always get what you want, when you want it. But yeah, that's cool. Okay, baby?"

"All right, now let's celebrate." I winked at her and put my left hand on her thigh. She smiled and discreetly parted her legs, and the split in her dress opened to reveal more of her thigh. My hand drifted a little higher and I felt heaven!

The rest of the evening was uneventful. Kree and I finished off the bottle of wine, feasted on Creole gumbo, talked and people-watched. At one point we spotted radio personality Frank Ski and members of his morning crew. They could barely make it to their table without people stopping them and shaking their hands.

When Kree started rubbing my back in small, then large circles, I knew it was time to go. Kree leaned over and whispered in my ear, "I want you to take me home now and fuck the living daylights out of me." Then she reached under the table and squeezed the merchandise. Alcohol always has that effect on her. With a smile on my face, I left a generous tip and grabbed her hand, "I'll be happy to oblige."

Needless to say, the remainder of the night was spent dancing between the sheets. As I entered the condo, I put on a couple of smooth CDs, grabbed another bottle of wine from the refrigerator and had Kree undressed before twenty minutes passed. After another glass of wine, Kree was ready. She was all over me, trying to get me to do her. Kree was begging for it. I love to mess with her when she is like this. I told her before I'd give her any, she had to do something for me.

In no time at all I was standing in the middle of our bedroom floor, naked, while Kree got down on her knees, opened her mouth wide, and sucked my dick like a pro. Afterward, Kree got her wish, two times. We both fell asleep with smiles on our faces, entangled in each other's arms.

Kree

"Mother, don't you think I've asked myself that same question over and over again? I don't know why Brice has this obsession with meeting them," I said as Mother ranted and raved relentlessly.

"What's the point? It doesn't make sense. There has to be some motivating factor."

"Brice claims he wants to make right some wrongs he caused in the past. Plus, he misses the brotherhood he and Christian shared. They literally grew up together!"

"Well, I don't like it one bit. And I'm going to go on record as saying so. You are just asking for trouble, girl."

"What am I supposed to do? If I don't go, he'll just go by himself."

"What do you mean, what are you supposed to do? Haven't I taught you anything? Child, use your womanly wiles. You always underestimate yourself. Do what you gotta do to get your way."

"Mother!"

"Mother, my ass. Don't give him any. Keep your legs closed. Don't even let him get a feel. It works wonders."

I didn't say anything in response to her solution. I quietly bit my fingernail.

"Kree, did you hear me? I can't believe you haven't learned anything from me. I had your daddy trained until the day he died, God bless his soul."

"Well, it doesn't work that way around here. Anyway, I'm somewhat curious about his ex."

"Well, be curious from a distance. Don't go up into her home, on her turf. Remember, she used to lie down with your husband, and Brice used to make love to her. If he's as good as you tend to make him out to be, then she hasn't forgotten either. You know women don't forget the ones who made them call out the name of Jesus and come at the same time. I know I haven't. I wish I could find old Freddy again now that your daddy is gone on. He's probably dead and buried, though."

I had to laugh at that. "Mother, you're a mess."

"No, I just tell it like I see it, and you'd better open up your eyes before it's too late."

"Mother, please! She's happily married to Christian."

Mother and I talked awhile longer as we always did, at least once, sometimes twice a week. My mother is a certified trip. She's off the chain. In fact, some of the things she says to me were more like a girlfriend talking to another girlfriend instead of mother to daughter. We've always been like that. She's like a best girlfriend. Maybe her being in her early fifties makes a difference.

When Daddy was alive, Mother kept him on his toes. My mother doesn't mince words or feelings; she keeps it real, too real at times. When Daddy passed away two years ago from colon cancer, I thought she would be lonely. I think she grieved for a minute, but it didn't take long for her to get back into the swing of dating. I wasn't surprised. Mother is a classy, cultured and beautiful lady. I was shocked at how many younger men tried to step to her.

When Brice and I returned to the States, we stopped by for a week's visit. Much to my surprise, Mother had a lover. I was thoroughly embarrassed when I woke up one night, walked into the kitchen to get a drink of water and heard them getting it on. Talk about loud; you would have thought the man was killing her. Miss Drama Queen. Yeah, my mother's a mess, but I love her to death!

I think she regrets that I'm not as aggressive as she'd like me to be. She says I let people walk all over me. Maybe she's right; maybe I do. Sometimes I wonder if I'm truly her daughter. However, I'm not about to cut my husband off from sex. If anything, our active sex life is bringing him home each night. I don't like some of the stuff he wants me to do in bed, but I do it anyway to please him. I'm not a fool. I see how women check him out from head to toe when we go out. Brice is fine! Women are bold! Some still won't turn away even when I catch them looking at my husband!

I got shudders from thinking about last night. It was so good, too good. Brice had me calling out to God, Jehovah and Sweet Mary, Mother of Jesus. It felt so wonderful that I started to cry on his shoulder, and shortly afterward we were at it again.

I hung up with promises to Mother that I'd be cautious and not go into this entire situation blindly. I'm not exactly thrilled about it either. I have a nagging feeling that these two people whom I have never met are going to change my world.

Mia

It's hard to believe it's already mid-April. The school year has flown by. It's going to be a typical hot summer in Atlanta, because the temperatures are already breaking record highs for spring. Each evening, after school, I changed into shorts to cook dinner. Christian calls them my Daisy Dukes. During the summer I live in shorts, halter tops and sandals. Anyone who knows me knows I'm definitely a no-frills type of person. My motto is, Less is better.

I never wear a lot of jewelry either. Usually I wear my wedding set, my diamond-stud earrings or my gold hoops and a cross pendant that Christian had given me years ago. The cross pendant is still my most cherished piece of jewelry because it belonged to his moms before she passed away. Christian is so sweet and thoughtful and always makes occasions special and memorable.

To say the last few weeks had been very hectic is an understatement. Preparing my students for final exams, report cards and end-of-school matters was keeping me too occupied to focus on our upcoming meeting with *him*. Christian seemed to be happy and wasn't dwelling on it either. Yet the date was fast approaching. He was still working crazy, long hours. So our hours together were cherished and few and far between. It still *amazes* me that we can talk for hours and hours on end about anything and everything and nothing at all. Lyric is growing more adorable each and every day. Yes, I'm biased. Our baby is our heart. Lyric has already learned how to manipulate her daddy to get her way. There is no doubt Christian loves her to no end. She is definitely Daddy's little girl.

Every evening he makes a special effort, no matter how tired he is, to play with her or read to her. It's their time together. On the nights

Christian got in too late, I'd found him on several occasions, simply staring at her as she slept. That always warms my heart to no end.

The other evening I had gone out to happy hour—which is something I rarely ever do—with another coworker, a fellow teacher, whom I considered a good friend. Sharon had been bugging me for months about going with her to Taboo. Since Christian was working late and Mama had agreed to keep Lyric for the evening, I decided to hang out and do the club thing. Sharon was pleased! The woman is a complete party animal. Talk about wild. Look in the dictionary under the word *wild* and you'll see a photo of Sharon.

She's a trip, but I *love* her just the same. Sharon is a tall—we're talking five-ten—big-boned woman, whom you usually heard before you saw. Yeah, she talks a lot of shit. Yet she's the most giving and free-hearted person I've ever met. She'd give you the shirt off her back. In my book, that's saying a lot.

It's amazing how Sharon manages two personalities. At work, she is a true professional adored by her students and praised by their parents and the faculty alike. Outside of work, the woman is about having a good time. Give her two drinks—her favorite is a Cosmopolitan—and she gets louder than loud. Whenever we go out, there's never a dull moment.

Thinking back, I don't know why Sharon chose me to be her best friend, because we're so opposite in lifestyles. I'm happily married with a child, and Sharon is independent, never married, with no children. She likes it that way; she can come and go as she pleases. The only thing she needs a man for is biweekly maintenance. If that fails . . . oh, well, she's good to go as long as she has AA batteries in stock. Those are her words, not mine. She says that her toy may have been a little impersonal, but it got the job done.

Sharon was hired my second year of teaching at Fairfield. She introduced herself to me in the teacher's break room and said she was going to be my new best friend, and the rest is history. Christian loves her like a sister and treats her like one too. They have a big-brother, little-sister relationship going.

Tonight she had me sitting in Taboo waiting for karaoke night, hosted by Wanda Smith. The place was crowded for a Tuesday night. Everyone was in a festive party mood. Sharon was nursing her second Cosmopolitan and I was working on my first screwdriver.

"Girlfriend, I'm glad I got you out of that house tonight. Tell Christian to let you come out for air once in a while. Y'all are like a li'l old couple, right under each other all the time."

We both laughed, as friends do, Sharon a bit too loud.

"I know, I know. I live a sheltered life; I need to get out more. I'll never be the life of the party like you are, girlfriend."

"Don't apologize; just sit back and take notes. I'm up for my bi-weekly maintenance and I'm badly in need of a sponsor." She laughed like it was the funniest line in the world.

"Girl, you're crazy." I laughed as I looked around at the crowd. Atlanta has such a wide gap in its women-to-men ratio. I think it's something like eight to one. Usually women outnumber the men at most events. I'd hate to be a single black female in Atlanta. But I don't have those worries. I have my Boo, and I knew exactly where he was tonight.

"Seriously, Mia, what's the deal? You haven't been yourself these last few weeks. You've been distracted about something. Come on; come clean," Sharon said with serious concern etched on her face.

"Is it that obvious?"

"Yes, it's that obvious. Something is going on. You're not my usual cheery friend that I've come to know and love."

"I don't know, girl. I guess I'm just nervous about this upcoming meeting."

"And you have every right to be. You're a better person than me. I would curse his ass out, tell him to fuck off, and keep on going. No love lost."

"I bet you would." I laughed.

"Hell, yeah, all that shit he put you through. Treating you like nothing. On second thought, no, actually, I'd get revenge and fuck him up."

We laughed at the possibility. "Seriously, Sharon, I'm having mixed feelings. I keep telling myself that I'm doing this for Christian, but deep down I want to see him again. I want him to see Christian and me together and see how happy we are. I want him to bear witness that he didn't ruin my life."

"Girl, I wish I could be a fly on your wall. What are you wearing?" she asked in all seriousness.

I looked at Sharon in disbelief. "I don't know. My wardrobe is the least of my worries."

"Think, Mia, think. You have to wear something real sexy. Something that shows him what he missed out on and can't touch again. Ever. You've got to be looking your best."

We both turned to the stage as a lady approached the stage dressed in black with hair down her back like Diana Ross. She took the microphone and announced that she was going to sing "Fallin' " by Alicia Keys.

My thoughts drifted back to Brice while Sharon gave her full attention to the stage. It's amazing that we made it through two and a half years of marriage. Brice was a definite control freak, and I was his number one controlee.

Looking back, I loved Brice with everything I had—and then some. I was young, naive, and probably had some unrealistic views about love and marriage. I thought my love for Brice could solve all problems, resolve all our conflicts. Unfortunately, our problems were too deep for my love alone. In the bitter end, my heart was broken beyond repair, and a part of me, that part deep, deep down, was forever lost.

Brice was like a chameleon. On one hand, he could be so loving, so romantic and devoted to my every need. Yet, at the toss of a coin, his temper, possessiveness and jealousy would overshadow everything else. It was his way or no way. Brice ran our household with an iron grip. His word was law. I tried to deal with it because I loved him. I did what he wanted, when he wanted, where he wanted and how he wanted. In return I received his love. However, that wasn't enough. It just wasn't enough. When his paranoia would come into play, I suffered from his beatings.

Brice never trusted me around men or women. I admit I used to be a bit of a flirt. Brice felt some man was going to steal me away, and the females, in his opinion, were just bad influences on me. So I didn't have a life other than with him. For me, that wasn't enough.

If I didn't do something, anything he wanted, I suffered. If I did something that was a figment of his imagination, I suffered. Either way, I lost. Brice, at one point, totally controlled my existence. That crazy muthafucka would make me strip down out of my underwear so that he could smell my coochie to make sure I hadn't slept with anyone. He would hit me one moment and, in his next breath, turn around and make the sweetest love to me. It's amazing how some good loving will make a woman stay around much longer than she should.

Throughout history, women have stuck around with the bad boy, the one who shows them no love, no respect, no wining and dining, no nothing. We stick around because we don't want to give up their boning us. We can get screwed by any man, but we find one who has skills and knows how to fine-tune our body like a violinist tuning his instrument and we don't want to give him up.

Our cycle continued far too long. Some of the shit that man made me do . . . And I did it for him. Don't get me wrong: When he was good, Brice was very good. I can't deny that he made me happy. Unfortunately, there were far too many unhappy times. Sad to say, it took my ending up in the hospital after he beat the shit out of me for me to literally see the light.

Throughout all of this, there was Christian—my one true light. I had his strong shoulders to lean on. Christian was my sounding board and true friend. It's true that we have no control over whom we love. The heart doesn't know. Before I knew it, I was in love with Christian. It's a different love, but a real love. A true love. A love that has evolved because of circumstances.

Brice was a love that I breathed for. Now he was coming back into my life. After five years, I haven't forgotten him. I still remember his masculine smell, his voice whispering in my ear in the throes of passion. I remember his strong hands touching me in intimate places, his lips caressing my body as he went inside me. I remember how he moved inside me and remember how he made me feel when he looked deep into my eyes as I called out his name over and over.

Sharon brought me back to reality with her loud laughter.

"Mia, you haven't heard a word I've said, have you?"

"What? I didn't hear—"

"That's obvious. You are in your own little world over there. If I wanted to come here alone—"

"Okay, okay, what did I miss?" I asked before she went on and on about how I was neglecting her.

"You see the tall, dark-skinned guy over in the far corner?" She boldly pointed him out.

"Yeah?"

"Well, he's the maintenance man for this week. Sexy has been giving me the eye all evening. You just watch; I'm going to sample those goods."

Sharon and I talked, laughed and drank some more, compliments of Sexy, for another hour or so before I called it a night. True to form, before we walked out the door Sharon had Sexy's home, work, pager and cell numbers and a date for later in the week. Amazing. Girlfriend is unbelievable.

Christian

Brice and I were both quiet while we cruised down I-20 West and listened to V-103 on an early Saturday morning. It was like old times again, us back together again. Older and wiser.

Brice broke the silence. "Man, promise me you'll think about it. I'd love to bring you in as a partner. The Two Musketeers together again. Wouldn't that be a trip?" Brice said as we made our drive over to his parents' house.

"I can't make any promises, but I will think about it. It sounds like you have everything planned out to the letter. It would be a great opportunity."

"Well, what's the problem, my brotha?"

"Mia. Mia's the problem," I replied without looking in his direction.

"Man, you can handle Mia."

"Brice, I don't 'handle' Mia. We make major decisions together."

"Hold up. I didn't mean it like that. I'm just saying you can convince her that this is a once-in-a-lifetime opportunity. It's too good to pass up."

"I don't know; we'll see. I'm still trying to get her to think it's a good idea to meet with you. Let me get her used to one idea at a time."

"How's your pops doing, man?" I asked with deep concern. For years he was one of the only male figures I had in my life.

Brice looked at me out of the corner of his eye. "If you stopped by to see Moms more, you'd know for yourself, wouldn't you?"

"Brice, our situation is kinda awkward."

"Yeah, it is, but they never stopped loving you. Moms asks about you all the time. Even when I was in Germany, she'd tell me to call you and work through our problems. When I told her you were stopping by, she was ecstatic."

"Cool."

"But Pops, he's not doing that well. He has his good and bad days, with Moms right by his side."

"Of course. Your moms ain't going nowhere."

"You ain't never lied."

"How does she feel about this situation, our new lives?" I always felt Brice's mother thought I had betrayed Brice by marrying Mia. Therefore I stayed away.

"Christian, Moms knows I messed up bad. In fact, she predicted this would happen if I didn't straighten up. Moms always loved you like a son and Mia like a daughter. That didn't change. She wanted you both to be happy; if with each other, so be it."

"It's that simple, huh?"

"Man, only you're complicating it. You're happy and I'm happy. Kree is the wife I've always wanted. She does what I tell her to." With that statement, Brice started laughing. I wasn't too sure if he was serious.

"Well, five years ago, you could have killed me with your bare hands." I glanced back out the window.

"Five years ago I was a different man. I've changed. I hurt a lot of people, but that was then; this is now."

"Yeah, this is now."

We rode, turning down a few secondary roads, passing familiar sights, in a comfortable silence while music played on the radio station.

"What does Kree think about this little reunion?" I asked Brice.

"She doesn't," he said nonchalantly.

"Doesn't what?" I was confused.

"Doesn't think. Kree does what I tell her to. There isn't any room for questioning anything."

"Man, you never cease to amaze me. Unbelievable." I laughed.

"Christian, I'm sorry if my views about marriage and relationships don't agree with yours."

"To each his own. If Kree is cool with that, more power to you."

"And she is. Women won't admit it, but they get off having a strong man telling them what to do. They're like little children; they have to have rules to follow. They like for real men to handle things. Take control."

"Yeah, right. Tell that to all these independent, black women right here in Atlanta. They'd think that bullshit you're spouting is something straight out of caveman days and that you're a mental-ward escapee."

"Man, you can have any of these so-called independent women. Next they'll be thinking they have balls and dicks too."

"Man, you are crazy! I mean crazy. We'll just agree to disagree." I threw up my hands in a truce.

"That's right. When I tell Kree to jump, she'd better ask how high." He laughed at his own joke. "Just kidding."

Once again, I wasn't too sure whether Brice was kidding or not.

About ten minutes later we pulled up in front of the two-story brick house that was my home years earlier. Pleasant memories flooded my mind and hit me square in the face. I slowly got out of the car and followed Brice up the walkway to the front door.

"Man, this still looks the same. Some things never change. God, this takes me back."

Before we could even ring the doorbell, Vivica, Brice's moms, opened the door with a smile that could melt the hardest of hearts.

"Christian, baby, come here and give me a big hug and kiss," she said with outstretched arms.

I couldn't help but smile and oblige as I wrapped my arms around her petite body. This was the lady who was like a second moms to me after mine had died. Vivica had aged gracefully, with salt-and-pepper hair that was pinned up into a bun at the back of her neck.

"Boy, I've missed you so much. Don't you ever stay away like that again. You hear me?" She gave me another hug and looked me over.

"I've missed you too, and I hear you, Mrs. Matthew."

"Mrs. Matthew?" she asked with confusion on her face.

"I hear you, Moms."

"That's better. You look good; you look happy. Now come on in this house."

When we finally made our way in, Brice spoke. "Oh, I bring Christian by and he gets all the love. No hellos for your dear, beloved son."

"Is that the son who was supposed to come by the other night with his wife for dinner?" she asked in a teasing voice.

"Moms, you know this business has me coming and going. There is never enough time. Anyway, I called to cancel." Brice kissed her on the cheek. "Where's Pops?" he asked.

"Oh, he's sleeping. He sleeps less and less at night. At bedtime he is so restless. So during the day, he naps. Christian, make yourself at home while I check on our dinner."

As soon as she said that, I smelled the mouthwatering aromas drifting into the living room from the kitchen. Vivica could throw down on some country cooking. If memory served me right, I was sure she had a big pot of collard greens with okra, fried chicken or baked ham, corn bread, fried corn and tomatoes, iced tea and some type of dessert—probably sweet potato pie.

I walked around the living room, picking up photos of Brice and me as preteens, teenagers and young adults. So many good memories surfaced. Brice was channel-surfing with the remote, trying to find a game on TV.

"Hey, Moms, I'm going upstairs to check on Pops."

"Okay, baby. Christian, come in the kitchen and sit with me," Vivica called.

I walked into the cozy kitchen to find Vivica standing at the stove stirring some collard greens in a big black pot as she checked on some corn bread in the oven. I smiled.

"Sit down, baby."

"Yes, ma'am."

"How's Mia?"

"She's fine, busy with school. You know the school year is almost over."

"You tell her to come see me sometime. Both of you."

"Okay, I will."

"I mean it."

I nodded my head.

"Christian, you've always been like a son to me. I love you, baby, and I've missed you."

"Thank you, same with me."

"You take good care of Mia. She deserves some happiness, and I know you can give her that and vice versa."

"Moms, that means so much to me." I walked over to give her a big hug.

"Christian, you and Mia have always had my blessings. Brice . . . I love him and he's my only son, but I also know right from wrong. He wanted to strip that girl of her spirit. He wanted a trophy wife. You know, someone who looked pretty on his arm and doted on him. What he did to that child was wrong. He knows my feelings all too well on that subject."

I just nodded as she placed a small sampling of her fried corn in front of me.

"I hope he does better with this new wife, Kree. She's a looker and just as sweet as can be."

I nodded with my mouth full of food.

"Have you met her yet?"

"No, ma'am, not yet. I've only seen a photo of her."

"She looks like . . ."

We heard Brice walking down the stairs, so Vivica changed the subject and winked at me.

"What's smelling so good in here?" He checked the pots and pans assembled on the stove.

"Boy, if you don't get your hands and nose out of my food with your greedy self . . . Sit down like Christian and I'll give you something to tide you over till dinner."

I had to laugh. Nothing had changed. This was typical Vivica-and-Brice interaction. The love was definitely there between mother and son.

"Oh, Pops woke up and said he was hungry."

"That man may be under the weather, but he hasn't lost that appetite."

She started to fix him a plate and asked Brice, "Where's Kree today?"

"She's over at the salon getting her hair done."

"Well, has she found a job yet? Didn't you or she say she has a fine arts degree?"

"Yes, she does, but my wife doesn't work. Her job is to be my wife. That's Kree's full-time job." Brice looked in my direction.

"Sometimes, baby, that's not enough," Vivica said with a sudden sadness in her sparkling eyes.

Brice and I spent a relaxing day at my second home. We talked, did some minor repairs in the upstairs bathroom, watched the game, and had a delicious meal. Of course, Vivica insisted on serving second helpings. So after dinner we were stuffed as we reclined on the sofa and love seat in the living room. I had come home. It felt good.

It was hard seeing the toll Alzheimer's had taken on Brice's pops when he was brought downstairs. He didn't say much, just kinda sat there and stared. I don't even think he recognized me. He responded to Vivica, though. It was all so sad and unfortunate. It made me realize how lucky I was to have a beautiful, loving wife and an adorable baby girl. It's funny how far I have come. Years ago, having a family and settling down was nowhere in my definition of a happy life. Now a happy life couldn't exist without Mia and Lyric. I'd be lost.

I haven't been spending much time with Kree lately. I usually rise early and return home late each evening. So, I'd called Kree thirty minutes earlier and told her to meet me for lunch at this little café I'd discovered. It looked like a lot of other customers had discovered it too. The place was packed with a loud lunch crowd. I was seated where I could watch the front entrance.

Kree hadn't arrived yet, probably because the traffic getting into Midtown at lunchtime was horrendous. So I sat, waited, drank my black coffee and thought about my conversation with Christian a couple of days earlier.

I knew Christian had mellowed out over the years, mainly since marrying Mia. I guess some would say he had matured in a number of ways. I couldn't believe my man was a daddy. Hell, Christian used to be a wild man who liked some wild women. I was usually right there with him at some bar or club. Christian and I definitely sowed our wild oats and then some. Those were the days! I could tell some stories that people wouldn't believe. They'd think I was making it all up, but now . . . things are different—for both of us.

I still feel that my boy condemns my views on marriage and relationships. To each his own. That's, at least one of the reasons why Mia and I didn't make it. Mia was too damn independent. I couldn't get her to understand that I was the man of my house—not her, me. Oh, but she soon learned. It took tapping that ass a few times. Mia wasn't about to run me! I put her ass on lockdown and that was that. I'm not proud of how I handled matters, but, regardless, my views haven't changed.

Kree, on the other hand, knows the deal. And she likes it, no complaints. As long as I provide the lifestyle she wants, then hey, Kree's cool. In the years we've been married, Kree and I have only had a few arguments. In the end, Kree cries and backs down. I know that crazy mother of hers is always trying to give her advice, but like I said, Kree knows the deal. I still say that's why her pops is dead and buried in an early grave; Kree's mother drove him crazy. I'm not about to put up with that type of shit. Hell, no!

As I picked up my cup to take another sip of coffee, Kree arrived and looked around for me. When she spotted me, I smiled. My wife is a beautiful, sexy woman. I admired her as she strolled the short distance over to my corner booth. Judging by the heads that were turning to stare at her as she walked by, I knew that to be the truth.

Today Kree was dressed in a floral-design silk dress, hanging slightly above the knee, that was hitting all the right places as she sashayed over. She pushed her hair behind her right ear, a habit she had along with biting her nails. I noticed the tiny pearl earrings she had on. They were the ones I had given her for our first wedding anniversary.

There was a time when seeing men staring at my wife would have upset me, made me mad as hell. Now I take it as a compliment to me. Other men could caress her with their eyes and imagine how she'd feel in their arms, but at night, she lay down in my bed, in my arms.

"Hey, baby. That traffic was horrible," she said, bending down to give me a quick peck on the cheek.

"Come here, girl, and give me a real kiss," I said playfully.

This time, I gave her a real kiss with tongue and all, and I made a point of patting her ass before she sat down beside me in our booth. I could feel the drooling tongues and lustful eyes.

I smiled. "Me and your room of admirers think you look great today."

"What admirers?"

"Look around, baby. Check 'em out. Don't you see the salivating tongues lying on the floor? See, I told you, you aren't observant at all."

Kree looked around and just blushed.

"Well, they can look, but they can't touch. Only you."

"And it had better stay that way," I said in all seriousness as I looked deep into her eyes.

I caught the look in Kree's eyes that said she realized I was serious. She coughed and looked down.

I signaled to the waiter when we were ready to order. He quickly took our orders, because I knew what we wanted. This was supposed to be one of the best Cuban restaurants in the area. I'd eaten here twice before and the food was excellent.

"Did you honor my request?"

"What request are you referring to, baby?" Kree asked, playfully rubbing my arm.

"My request from my last phone call less than an hour ago. How soon we forget."

"I'm sorry, but I did forget; refresh my memory. Come on, talk to me, baby."

"Oh, you want to play games, Kree?" I asked in mock anger.

"No, baby, just give me a hint."

"Okay, come closer and I'll whisper it in your ear."

Kree slid over closer to me.

I bent down and moved her hair away from her ear. "I requested that my beautiful wife indulge me in my fantasy."

"Go on, I'm listening." She grinned a seductive smile.

"I asked that my wife leave the underwear at home and show me her pussy, since I haven't seen it in over a week."

"Oh, I see. Is it your wife's fault that you're too tired every night? All you want is sleep. Is that her fault?"

"No, baby, it isn't."

"All work and no play makes Brice a dull boy."

"I know, baby."

"Well, I have a surprise for you." She slid over closer to me and caressed my face. "Oops, I dropped my fork; be a gentleman and pick it up for me."

I smiled and bent down to reach under the table to retrieve her fork.

"Do you like what you see?"

"Looks like paradise to me."

She slowly inched her dress up and spread her legs. She'd honored my request after all. "Well, pick up my fork and come back to the table, because our waiter is on his way over," she anxiously stated.

I picked up her fork and slid back next to Kree just as our waiter arrived with our entrées. Kree and I both looked at each other and burst out laughing. The Cuban waiter looked from one to the other like we were both escaped lunatics from the local nuthouse. After he left, we enjoyed our lunches, chatted and, every now and then, we'd look at each other and burst out laughing all over again.

After lunch, I did something I hadn't done in years. Kree had turned me on so much that I couldn't go back to work yet. I drove her over to a nearby park and found a secluded spot, which was easy, since it was the middle of a workday. I leaned her against an oak tree, pulled up her dress, and handled my business until I got enough of what I'd been missing.

Kree

Okay, I'm bored silly. My life has to consist of more than exercising, trips to the mall and gym, watching TV, playing Miss Homemaker and pleasing Brice at night. Speaking of Brice, he's happy, very happy. He's following his dreams, and things are quickly coming together. However, sometimes I feel that his dreams don't involve or include me. I feel like I'm losing him.

When we first moved to Georgia, things were cool because Brice spent more time with me. He drove me around, helped me to learn my way around the city and get a feel for Southern living. I had my own personal tour guide. So I never had the opportunity to be bored, but now . . . now I'm bored.

Brice is never home, yet he expects me to be here at his beck and call. He always has me running around doing errands for him: Pick up this, call this person, check on this. I feel like his glorified secretary instead of his wife.

In Germany, I had things to do because the American wives of the marines stuck together. Some of those women became like sisters to me, and I loved their children dearly. I still kept in touch with a few of them.

I want to do something with dance. There are several studios and clubs that need dance instructors. Even though it's just part-time, the manager of the gym where I work out asked me to teach an aerobics class. I know Brice is going to say no at first, but he has to understand how bored I am and allow me to work. It's only part-time, and I'll be here in the evening when he arrives home. It shouldn't be a problem.

Believe it or not, Brice actually arrived home a little early today, and I was ready. I had prepared one of his favorite meals: smothered pork chops and baked potatoes with green beans and a Caesar salad on the side. I had even gone out and picked up a chocolate chip cheesecake from Mick's.

I had already showered and sprayed on his favorite perfume. My hair was loose, in small curls. I had on my sexiest lingerie with a matching robe and slippers. Maybe some of Mother's conversation was rubbing off on me, because I was trying to use my womanly wiles to get my way.

Things started out smoothly. When Brice walked in the door, I met him with a deep, passionate kiss. I know I looked good, because a lustful look immediately appeared on his face. I handed Brice a glass of wine and told him to undress. I had a hot bath ready and waiting for him. Brice just looked at me with raised eyebrows and walked down the hallway.

I followed him into our bedroom. He started to take off his clothes and commented that dinner smelled good. Once in the bathroom, I sat on the toilet seat and watched as he undressed his magnificent body. Brice's body is gorgeous; I could sit and just stare at it all day. When he flexed to pull off his shirt, I saw his bulging muscles, and when he pulled down his pants and the underwear came off, his jimmy was semi-erect.

After Brice got in the tub, I sat on the edge and washed his back in gentle circular motions. I made my first mistake by asking him about the job before he was fully relaxed. He hadn't even finished his first glass of wine.

"No, Kree, absolutely no. Hell no," Brice screamed.

"Tell me one good reason why not, baby?" I whimpered.

"Kree, when we first married, I told you I didn't want a wife who worked," Brice screamed. He finished bathing himself and prepared to get out of the tub.

"Oh, I didn't know it was set in stone. I didn't know it was a legal, binding agreement. Anyway, this isn't like really working. It's only teaching a class a few hours a day. I'd be home before you got here."

Brice wrapped a large purple towel around his waist and began to rub lotion all over his body, ignoring me.

"You should be glad I'm contributing to the household fund. It's going to be tight until the business is up and running," I cried, still trying to make my case.

"Kree, let me worry about the money and providing for our household. You don't worry about it. The change you'd make from that place wouldn't make or break us," Brice hissed as he continued to look at himself in the mirror. He began to brush his teeth. "Anyway, I don't want my wife working half-naked around all those horny men who are in and out of that place."

By now I was standing behind him with my arms wrapped around his waist and my head resting on the center of his back. I made sure my breasts brushed up against him a couple of times.

"Baby, mostly women take the class."

Brice spat out the mint-flavored toothpaste and rinsed out his mouth with water.

"I don't care. You're not doing it. I knew this whole setup was so you could get something out of me."

"It wasn't even like that, baby. I just want to make you happy. You're never home now, and I wanted tonight to be special and relaxing for you."

"Whatever, Kree. Today has not been a good day. It's been setback after setback. So coming home and listening to your damn mouth is not helping matters," Brice said as he massaged his creased forehead.

I made my second mistake of the evening. "But Brice . . ." I started to say.

"Kree, didn't I tell you to shut the fuck up? What part of that don't you understand?"

"I know that this—"

What happened next took place in slow motion. Brice turned around and grabbed me by the shoulders and slammed me into our bathroom wall. "N-O, Kree. I said *no* and I don't want to hear another muthafuckin' word about it. Do you understand me or do I have to make you understand?"

I just stood there, shaking like a leaf and staring at him in disbelief. "Kree, *do you understand me?* Answer me!"

By now, his towel had fallen to the tiled bathroom floor and his nakedness was pressed up against me. I felt totally violated. I couldn't get my brain to tell my vocal cords to speak the words he wanted to hear.

"Kree, I'm going to ask you one more time if you understand me. I suggest you answer me," he barked with fury in his glazed eyes. He held my chin in a viselike grip and forced me to look at him.

"Yes, Brice, I understand," I whimpered, starting to cry uncontrollably.

"Don't start that crying, Kree. You know I hate that shit! Damn, I didn't need this tonight!" Brice let go of my chin and bent down to pick up his towel. "Now clean up your face. When you come out, fix my plate."

I got a warm washcloth to rinse my tears away and noticed the beginnings of small bruises on my shoulders. I forced myself to stop crying before Brice came back with all his fury.

"Kree, I'm hungry! I'm waiting for you to fix my plate," Brice shouted from the next room.

I jumped at the sound of his voice.

"Kree?"

"I'm coming, Brice. Just a minute."

When I made it to the kitchen, I had securely wrapped my robe around my gown and I couldn't look at him. I proceeded to fix his plate while Brice sat at the table and read the newspaper. No words were exchanged, no apologies exclaimed.

I placed his hot plate in front of him and was getting ready to leave. "You're not eating?"

"I'm not hungry." I looked at the floor and bit my nail down further.

"Come on, baby, sit down and eat with me." He folded up the paper and placed it to the side.

"Okay." I nervously twisted a piece of my hair behind my ear. I put a small portion of food on my plate and sat down quietly across from him. I focused all my attention and energy on my plate and making it through dinner. My perfect evening had gone straight to hell.

Brice continued to eat and look at me while I attempted to chew my food. I didn't dare look up.

"Kree, I didn't mean to hurt you, but you know my feelings about having a stay-at-home wife. When we have babies, I want their mother at home."

Still looking down, I said, "I know." I wanted to say, *We don't have babies yet. So what's your point?* However, I knew the deal by now. I still remembered the first time he hit me early in our marriage. Over in Germany, I had arrived home late from a day of shopping to find a fuming Brice sitting on the sofa, eating a cold sandwich and drinking a beer. Angry words were exchanged, tears were shed by me, and I ended up with a split lip and promises from an apologetic Brice that he would never, ever hit me again.

"Kree, look at me. You can't stand to look at me now? Believe me, I didn't mean to hurt you."

I glanced up.

Brice looked like a wounded animal. I forced myself to give a plastic smile. "Okay, baby, I believe you."

That seemed to make him happier and less tense. "Kree, you don't have to cover up your body from me. Get up and pull off your robe."

I stared at him for a few seconds in disbelief, not moving, and Brice patiently waited. Something in his eyes told me to do what he asked.

"Okay." I slowly stood up to untie my robe and place it on the adjacent kitchen chair. The flimsy material of my short gown didn't cover up too much. Now I felt self-conscious with my nakedness.

Brice looked me up and down with appreciation. I guess he ignored the bruises that were very prevalent now.

"Nice. I love to see you in that."

We continued the remainder of our dinner in silence. I don't know what was going through Brice's mind, but I was thinking that, once again, he was making me feel like a whore. Every now and then Brice would ask me something and I would answer. It was all a blur.

When Brice finished his dinner, I jumped up to take his plate into the kitchen, scrape it off and place it in the dishwasher. I planned to go to bed and get away from Brice for the remainder of the night.

As I was walking by, Brice grabbed me gently by the hand. "Come here, Kree. Where are you going in such a hurry?" He pulled me onto his lap and intertwined his fingers with mine.

I sat down with my entire body frozen. Stiff.

"Relax, baby, I'm not going to hurt you; loosen up." He gently massaged my neck and back in circular motions.

Brice looked at me curiously for a second, then tilted my head to his with his hand, forcing his tongue into my mouth and pulling me into him.

Brice rubbed his strong, firm hands between my legs and kissed my neck and breasts until a soft moan escaped my lips. He tongued me down with deep, passionate kisses and gently sucked and squeezed my breasts and nipples as they responded to his touch. My gown was down at my waist now.

"Yeah, that's my baby. Close your eyes and give in to the good feelings. Doesn't that feel good?" he repeated over and over while his fingers probed and prodded.

Even though I didn't want to enjoy it, my body betrayed me. Brice swept me up into his arms like his property and carried me into our bedroom.

At one point he turned my chin to make me look at him, deep into his light brown eyes.

"Kree, come for me, baby. Give in to it; come for me." Faster, deeper, faster, harder he went. A volcano was rising. Bubbling. Erupting. It was amazing. Suddenly I felt this warm sensation engulf my entire body and my legs started trembling. At his command I came for him, hard. Brice never took his eyes off me. I shuddered uncontrollably beneath him as he stroked my hair and face. With images of Brice triumphantly smiling down at me, I fell sound asleep.

Mia

"Okay. I'm okay. I couldn't be better. I'm fine. Inhale . . . exhale . . . breathe through your nose. It's natural to be nervous. He doesn't control me. He can't intimidate me any longer." I repeated this three times softly to myself as I pulled outfit after outfit from my walk-in closet and dresser drawers. Too tight, too conservative, too short, too sexy . . .

The big reunion night had finally arrived after several delays. Lyric had gotten an ear infection and Christian had gone in to work unexpectedly, etc. . . . Tonight was the night; we couldn't put it off any longer. It was showtime! Lights, camera, action!

Christian had been dressed long ago. He chose a simple pair of tan slacks with a light-colored, lightweight pullover sweater. Christian was looking completely casual, laid-back and relaxed with his recently trimmed hair and goatee. This wasn't fazing him one bit. I had finally gotten him out of the house for a short time. I gave him and Lyric kisses and sent him on his way to drop her off at Mama's for the night.

I didn't need to be any more nervous than I already was, and Christian's watching and rushing me was not helping matters. After leaving Mama's, he had instructions to pick up our Greek salads and the shrimp and lobster party platters from a little gourmet shop near Midtown. The bottles of wine were already chilling in the refrigerator, and our house was immaculate. It was so clean you could literally eat off the floor. It should be; I had spent last night cleaning it from top to bottom. Nervous energy.

I felt like a giddy teenager getting ready for her first big date. My stomach was full of butterflies and nervous flutters. It wasn't that I was looking forward to this; it was that I didn't know what to expect from tonight. If memory served me correctly, anything was possible with Brice.

Christian had finally informed me that he and Brice had met and talked weeks earlier. I wasn't surprised, and, amazingly, I wasn't even upset. I knew my Boo missed him, and my love for Christian overcame any anger I may have felt. Now Brice had my palms sweaty, had me pacing back and forth and basically acting like a lunatic, with my stack of clothes getting higher and higher on our king-size bed. I couldn't decide if I wanted to go casual, dressy, in between or what. I didn't know how to dress or even how to act. I was at a serious loss, but Brice had always had that effect on me.

Finally I stopped, chilled and reflected after a frantic call to Sharon. She said one sentence to me and I was empowered: "Girl, don't give him your power." With that one line, I hung up with a smile on my face and Sharon's advice in mind—to make him sorry for what he couldn't have anymore.

After deciding to be myself, I chose to wear a denim wraparound knee-length skirt with a bright red knit wraparound top that tied on the side. It dipped a bit low in the front, but it had a built-in support bra and was comfortable. Tonight comfort was key.

Pleased that I had finally made a decision on my attire, I could relax for a minute. However, after glancing down at my watch, I decided I'd better get a move on because the magic hour was fast approaching. As my soothing bubble bath ran, I gave the living room one last going over. I strategically placed photos of Christian and me, and of Christian, Lyric and me, all happily enjoying our lives together, throughout the living room. I moved one of our wedding photos to the end table.

I placed the potpourri in containers and lit my scented candles—not because I was trying to create an intimate atmosphere or mood, but because I had discovered years earlier that candles relaxed me and the potpourri simply made the house smell great. A few minutes later I immersed myself in my soothing bathwater and listened to my Sade CD, the one with all her hits, on which she sings about the ups and downs of love gone wrong and loving someone too much: "Is It a Crime," "Sweetest Taboo."

I lay back against the tub, closed my eyes and wondered again if I was—if we were—making the right decision. Well, it was too late now. In another hour and fifteen minutes, according to the clock, *he* would reenter my life, a man I hadn't set eyes on in nearly five years. A man whom I had given everything I had to give and it still wasn't enough. Brice took, took and took. Sade had been there; she could relate. I could feel her pain through her music. I personally knew what it felt like to be a fool for love.

I finally toweled off, rubbed Tropical Nectar Victoria's Secret lotion all over my body, and sprayed on one of my favorite perfumes, Miracle. It was going to take a miracle to make it through this evening. By the time I heard Christian unpacking grocery bags in the kitchen, I had put the finishing touches on my hair and makeup. I loved my hair in this short, wavy style. It was low-maintenance. All I had to do was spray on some oil sheen, brush, fluff my fingers through it and go. My makeup consisted of a touch of Fashion Fair red lipstick and a hint of mascara on my already thick eyelashes. Sometimes I wore a little blush or eye shadow.

I took one last look at myself in the full-length mirror mounted on the closet door and smiled at my reflection. I must admit, I looked good. Glowing even. I was lucky after having Lyric; my body bounced right back. I still had perky breasts and a flat, tight stomach. I looked to the right, then turned to the left. Yeah, I looked *good.* Damn good! *Eat your eyes out, Brice. Your ass won't touch this again.* When I walked into the kitchen, Christian did a double take as he finished putting the food on one of our silver platters.

"Did you get everything, baby?" I put my arms around his waist from behind and squeezed hard.

"Yes, baby, everything on your list. Do you want to double-check?" he asked jokingly, squeezing me back.

"No, no, I believe you. I just want everything to be perfect." I rearranged some items on the platter. There was nothing like a woman's touch.

Satisfied with the arrangement of my platter, I checked on the wine and the cheesecake in the fridge again. Then I wiped off the counter, which was already clean, for the third time. I walked over to the sink to wash a juice glass that was in there, dried it off and placed it in the cabinet. Christian stood there the entire time, leaning against the counter, watching me move around like I had ants in my pants. Nervous energy.

"Mia, Mia. Baby, come here."

I slowly walked into his open arms and he embraced me with a kiss on the forehead. "Chill, baby. Be still; you're making me dizzy. Relax."

Christian and I both looked at our octagon clock on the wall at the same time. We still had another fifteen minutes or so before they arrived. "Please, Mia, go sit down. There's nothing left to do. Everything is perfect, baby."

I followed Christian's advice and had a seat at the far end of our love seat.

"Mia, your moms said not to pick up Lyric until after 2:00 tomorrow. They're going to morning church service at Bald Rock."

"Okay, baby," I responded, slightly distracted. Mama loved to dress Lyric up like a doll-baby in frilly dresses, take her to church and show off her granddaughter.

By now, Christian was next to me on the love seat.

"Remember, now, if you feel uncomfortable we don't have to go through with this."

"Okay, Boo, I remember." I smiled at him, "We can do this!"

Christian glanced at me out of the corner of his eye as I fiddled with the throw pillow on the sofa.

"Christian, you're here; there's nothing I fear, baby."

Christian and I talked for a few more minutes about our summer vacation plans, and I actually felt the tension easing itself slowly away and found myself relaxing. Christian did that to me; he relaxed me, made me feel secure and comfortable wrapped in his enduring love.

Roughly twelve minutes later, time stood still. The doorbell rang right on time. Brice always was prompt to a fault. My heart skipped a few beats, and I vaguely recall Christian smiling to reassure me and announcing that they were here.

Somehow I made it to the front door holding on to Christian's back pocket for dear life.

"You ready?"

My mouth was suddenly dry, so I just nodded my head because I was scared.

Christian opened the door to my past and I went back in time to five years earlier. To a time when Brice was my universe, the very air I breathed. He was my reason for waking up each morning. I heard the familiar voice and felt his overwhelming presence before I actually saw his face.

"What's up, partner?" Brice asked as he shook Christian's hand and pulled him into a hearty embrace, the kind good friends shared.

"Nothing, man, come on in. Make yourself at home."

Christian moved to the side and I saw Brice for the first time. Our eyes locked on each other at the same moment. It was a blast from the past. Feelings rushed forward. Memories. Flashes of conversation. Good times. Passion, much passion. Hands and fists connecting with flesh. Brice smiled that dazzling smile he used to save just for me, and somehow I managed to plaster a fake-ass smile all over my face as well.

I didn't know how to greet him, so I held out my right hand in an effort to shake his hand. Stupid, I know, so stupid. Brice smiled and pulled me into his arms for a warm embrace. He whispered in my ear, "Mia, you look as beautiful as ever. I've missed you."

He held me in his arms in a hug that lasted a bit too long, and I felt chills run up and down my arms. As I inhaled his cologne, I remembered the passion we used to share. When Brice slowly released me, I just stood there with that same wack smile still plastered all over my face. Then I remembered something—*Breathe.* I remembered to breathe. *Inhale, exhale, that's right; breathe, girl.*

In all the emotional excitement, I didn't see the young lady patiently standing in our doorway waiting for introductions until she softly cleared her throat.

Brice smiled again, the same smile he had just given me, and his eyes lit up. "Kree, come here, baby. Let me introduce you to some old friends."

Brice gently pulled his young wife by her arm and I was face-to-face with Kree—for the first time. Eye-to-eye. For a brief second I saw fear flash across her face.

I'm sure I must have stood there with my mouth wide-open for a minisecond. Kree looked like me. It was like looking at myself in the mirror, but five years younger. Sure, she had longer hair, much longer, was taller, not as thin as me, had fuller lips, but all in all, Kree could have been my baby sister. Didn't anyone else see this?

Kree must have noticed the resemblance as well because I saw her give me a quick once over, as women do, from my feet to my face, all within a few moments, sizing me up.

As I got my voice back and held out my hand in greeting, I said in my most sincere voice, "Hi, Kree, it's nice to meet you."

"Hi, Mia," was all she said as she gave me a limp, half-assed handshake without a hint of a smile on her full lips.

"Baby, this is Christian. This man here is like a brother to me," Brice exclaimed, putting his arm around Christian's shoulder and pulling Kree closer. It was like old times again. Well, not exactly. It was the same cast, almost, but a different script.

"Hi, Christian. It's so good to finally meet you face-to-face. I feel like I know you already because I've heard your name so often over the years." She gave Christian a dazzling smile and a huge hug as she pressed up against him.

I stood there and looked on in awe. I was already beginning not to like her. We all kind of stood in the foyer for a few seconds more, not knowing what to say or do after the initial greetings and introductions were over.

Finally Christian broke the awkward silence.

"Kree, Brice, make yourselves at home. Come on in. Have a seat."

I took Christian's hand as he followed behind them into the living room. Brice and Kree seated themselves on the sofa by the wall and Christian and I sat on the love seat. Because of the position of the love seat, I ended up sitting closest to Brice. It was overwhelming, to say the least, being that near to him after all those years. Brice looked great, though. The years had been too good to him. It was obvious that he was still working out. He looked to be in better form now than when we were married.

Dressed casually in linen pants and a matching shirt, he was too fine. Brice's hair was perfectly cut, mustache trimmed. He smelled good enough to eat, and he exuded sex appeal all over the place. It was seeping out of his pores. The years hadn't taken the edge off his arrogance either, because he was boldly checking me out from head to toe.

I watched out the corner of my eye as his eyes caressed me, lingering on my thighs and focusing on my chest. His eyes revealed that they liked what they saw. Brice kept checking me out while his wife sat there like a stone. Like she'd rather be anywhere but here. I could feel her pain.

"You guys have a lovely home. Very cozy and inviting," Brice said, glancing around.

Kree nodded in agreement.

"Thank you," Christian and I responded in unison.

"Yeah, we closed on our house about two years ago. Mia instantly loved it. All the credit goes to her; she did all the decorating herself."

I nodded my head in agreement.

"Does anyone want anything to drink? We have beer, wine . . ." Christian said.

"I'll take some wine, please," Kree stated, very ladylike and proper.

I silently rolled my eyes at Miss Black Barbie.

"Give me a brew, man."

"Mia?" Christian asked, pulling me up out of my evil thoughts.

"I'll have some wine too. Here, let me help you, baby."

"No, no, I'll get it. Relax."

Looking in Christian's direction, Kree asked, "Where is your bathroom?"

"Follow me; I'll show you. Mia, why don't you put on some music?" Christian rose from the sofa.

I looked from him to Brice and back to Christian again. If looks could kill, Christian would have been dead on the spot. As he wandered off to show Kree the bathroom and get our drinks, I was left alone with Brice. He had an amused smirk on his face, realizing my discomfort and heightened anxiety.

I quickly got up to turn on the CD player in the middle of the entertainment center. "Any requests?" I asked without turning around. I could feel his eyes boring into my back and ass.

I thought, *You won't be dippin' your spoon in this anymore. Look all you want.*

Brice answered, "Let's take it back. You got any Marvin Gaye, Aretha Franklin, any old school?"

"I'll check. I know Christian has just about anything you can name. They're here somewhere. I'll check the rack. He doesn't have his CDs arranged in any special way, so it's hard for me to find anything. Of course, he knows where everything is," I rambled on and on in nervous chatter.

As I stood there searching through the CD rack, I could still feel Brice's eyes on my ass, checking me out. It was making me nervous. I felt exposed.

"Mia, looks like you have put on a little bit of weight, in all the right places."

I turned, rolled my eyes and looked at him with no comment.

Brice laughed. "You look good, girl, but you always did. Christian must be treating you good."

"You're right about that." I kept searching for the CDs.

"Here, let me help you." In no time, Brice got up and was standing right behind me, looking over my shoulder, before I could protest. Brice is a tall man and I'm short and petite so it was like he was towering over me. I felt slightly intimidated and overwhelmed by his presence. I tried to move away, but he was blocking my path.

"You smell good; what do you have on?" He leaned down to sniff my neck and placed his hands on my bare shoulders. Instantly, goose bumps appeared on my arms and shoulders. Of course, Brice noticed.

Kree returned from the bathroom. She glanced from Brice to me and back to Brice. Kree found her seat back on the sofa and looked our way again, chewing on her nail. I found some old-school CDs and placed them in the player. Brice returned to his seat by his adoring wife. I noticed how attentive he was to her. He pushed a strand of hair out of Kree's face and caressed her left cheek with his thumb. He whispered something in her ear and she laughed in this high-pitched laugh. Brice touched her hand gently and played with her fingers.

It was interesting to watch my ex-husband being intimate with another woman. Yes, his touches to Kree were very intimate. Almost erotic. He touched her in the knowing way that a man touches his woman, a man sure of the effect his caresses have on her. Kree was eating it up. I knew in that instant that she'd do anything for him.

"Kree, how do you like Atlanta?" I asked, trying to play the happy-hostess role.

"It's cool. Yeah, the South is cool, but it doesn't matter where I am as long as I'm with Brice. This could be Alaska for all I care."

"Have you had the opportunity to see much of the city yet? MLK Center, the Apex Museum, Underground, Olympic Centennial Park?"

"Yeah, when we first moved here, Brice was my personal tour guide. We were all over this city." She looked lovingly at Brice. "Now I can get around pretty well."

I gave her another fake-ass smile and resisted the urge to throw up.

Just in the nick of time, Christian reentered with our drinks on a tray. I was going to be sick if Kree said "Brice this" or "Brice that" one more time. I swear, did the woman have her own damn identity?

I thought to myself that it was going to be a very long evening. I grabbed my drink and gulped it down in a few swallows. By the time Aretha Franklin's "I Never Loved a Man the Way I Love You" came on, I was feeling a light buzz. I could handle this. Yeah, I could even handle Brice's eyes on me, watching my every move. I could do this. Now I was invincible.

We decided to wait a little longer for dinner. No one was very hungry, and we chatted and caught up on one another's lives. About an hour had passed. I moved to the floor to relax. That was something I always did when Christian and I were at home. Brice followed suit with the pretense that he needed to stretch his long legs. Now he was right in my face, sipping on his second or third beer.

"Mia, I love your hair."

"Thank you."

"What made you cut it so short?" He reached over and ran his strong, firm hand casually through my hair. "It's you, sassy. Wouldn't you say so, Christian? Mia always was sassy."

"Yeah, you could say that, and that's just one of the many reasons why I love her so."

I missed most of what Christian had said, because I couldn't believe Brice had run his fingers through my hair. Who the hell did he think he was? "I needed a change, a fresh start. You know, out with the old, in with the new."

Brice nodded and laughed. He looked at me like he was privy to a private joke.

"I prefer for Kree to wear her hair long."

"What does Kree prefer?" I asked, looking in her direction.

Kree was sitting in the same exact spot on the sofa in her crisp but expensive magenta silk dress, sipping her wine like a true black American princess.

"I like what Brice likes; he likes it long. So I keep it that way for him. I love to please my husband."

"Again, what do *you* like?" I asked with a serious scowl on my face.

"I like it long too. It's more feminine. No offense, Mia, but I could never wear your style; it's too boyish."

"Um-hmm."

"Yeah, Mia, Kree likes to please her man." Brice stared at me in obvious amusement.

Christian saw that I was fuming inside. He knew the expression and tried to change the subject: "Kree, Brice tells me you have a performing arts degree."

With this, her face broke out into a glowing smile.

"Yes, I majored in modern dance and theater. I love to dance. In fact, when Brice and I met I was out dancing at a popular club in Germany."

"Cool. That's real cool."

I interrupted. "If you have this great passion for dance, why aren't you using your talent and degree, Kree?"

From the expression that crossed her face, I knew I had hit a nerve. I smiled inside.

Brice took over. "Kree wants to be a traditional wife. See, that's what's wrong with families these days. Both parents are working, doing their own thing, and so are the kids. They all live in the same house, under the same roof, but that's about it. They don't know each other. The children are raising themselves. That's how these kids can build bombs, go shoot up their teachers, schools and anybody else they don't like. We are going to raise our kids the right way, by being there for them, nurturing them, teaching them morals and values. Our children are going to know we are always there for them."

"Well, Mia does a great job of balancing our family life, raising Lyric and teaching. I think a good balance can be achieved if you work at it," Christian stated, rushing to my rescue.

I reached for another glass of wine. I was proud of Christian for coming to my defense. How dared Brice imply I wasn't raising Lyric in the proper manner and being a good mother?

"Christian, you'd better close out Mia's bar tab. You know how she gets when she's had too much to drink."

All eyes fell on me, and everyone thought it was funny except for me. In reality, I never drank a lot, because I grew up watching Mama drink her life away after Daddy had died. Back then I didn't want to end up like her, an alcoholic. When Brice and I were married, I rarely drank, and he knew that.

There was a time in our marriage, toward the end, when my drinking had put me in a compromising position with this soldier named Malcolm. I was drunk and Malcolm tried to take advantage of my impaired state. I paid dearly for that mistake at Brice's hands.

We made it through dinner without any more inside remarks. Christian was an attentive, charming host. Brice talked about his tour of duty in Germany, his new business venture and, of course, sports. When I asked her questions, Kree answered with one-word answers. Other than that, she didn't say too much of anything—to me, anyway. She was more like Brice's decorative piece, who couldn't keep her hands off him. Kree was constantly touching him somewhere. Every now and then, I'd catch her staring at Christian or directing some comment only to him.

Much later, we were all sitting around in the living room after a good meal and excellent wine. We were all mellow, lying back against soft sofa cushions and listening to Marvin Gaye sing of the problems of the world. The candles were burning low by now and we were chillin'. Christian had his head in my lap while I stroked his eyebrows, and Kree was all but attached to Brice.

I don't know who suggested playing charades to liven things back up, and I can't remember who suggested being on teams. The teams consisted of me and Brice, and Kree and Christian. Some of the movies we acted out called for a little too much touchy-feely for me. However, it was all in fun. Even Kree loosened up some, and I saw a glimpse of her true self. I think if I had met her under different circumstances, we could have been friends. Under the present circumstances, I got the sense that Kree felt I was a threat. Christian and Brice were both being competitive and took the game a little too seriously. When it was all said and done, Christian and Kree won by one game.

I must say, the evening ended on a high note. We were all laughing. Even though Kree and I weren't bosom buddies, she did seem to like Christian, and being in the same room with Brice wasn't freaking me out any longer. I was proud of myself and couldn't wait to tell Sharon all the details. In fact, I knew she'd be calling me first thing the next morning. As the evening came to a close, we made plans to meet again real soon.

Christian

"**M**r. Pope, did you hear what I just said?"

"What? I'm sorry. Repeat that again," I said to Michael, who was one of my best security guys. He had a knack for sensing trouble and being on top of things.

"The sixth-floor situation was a false alarm. The unidentified, suspicious white male worked on that floor. He's new, just started today, and wasn't known by Mrs. Shawford."

We both chuckled and shook our heads. Mrs. Shawford, from the sixth floor, was notorious for spotting so-called suspicious characters in the building or even in the parking garage. She was also known for being totally wrong in most instances. My staff received so many calls from her that they knew her voice now.

My place of employment was in the center of a major street in the heart of Midtown. Our multilevel building housed a banking center, businesses, and several shops and restaurants. Therefore, there was always an assortment of people in and out for various reasons. There were also a lot of street people who hung out in and around our building. The last couple of months had been rather busy with people walking in off the street, accessing floors without the use of scan cards and stealing unsecured laptops, wallets and purses. The perpetrators would attempt to walk right out the door with the laptops in their gym bags or briefcases. My staff had tightened up on security, and every call, even from Mrs. Shawford, had to be taken seriously.

"Good job, man. Just write it up in your report."

"Sure thing," he said as he walked over to the drawer of files against the wall.

I had been too caught up in my daydreaming to hear Michael when he had entered my small, cramped office space. Luckily I didn't spend too much time in there. I was attempting, however unsuccessfully, to catch up on some much-needed paperwork when thoughts of Saturday filled my mind.

It was the Monday after our little get-together, and I hadn't had the chance to speak with Brice. This was the first time I'd even had the opportunity to sit down. To think. Sunday had been spent doing the family thing after picking up Lyric. Mia and I had gone to a nearby park and let her run around and play for a while.

I felt everything went down cool. I admit, it was awkward at first, but after that initial phase, everybody had a good time. Mia didn't say too much after they left, but she was smiling. So . . . that was a good sign!

As for me, it was weird, if that's the right word to use, seeing them, Brice and Mia, together again. I noticed how my man kept checking out my woman whenever he thought I wasn't looking. Did I feel threatened? No. Jealous maybe, weird yes.

I had high expectations for our get-together. I wanted this to be the beginnings of a new beginning. I admit I missed having Brice and his family in my life. I realized that the day we went to visit his moms. For a minute, even though I didn't tell Mia, I was skeptical of our little reunion. Mia and Kree didn't exactly hit it off. It was ice-cold up in there for a while. However, the more wine consumed, the better the situation got. Barriers started tumbling down.

Kree, just as I assumed, was a beautiful woman. I wouldn't expect any less from Brice's woman. And Brice had her where he wanted her—wrapped around his little finger. It was obvious that if Brice said jump, Kree would say how high. I don't know how Brice did it. Women would do anything for that man. The tales I could tell. Stuff people wouldn't even believe, stuff I wouldn't believe if I hadn't witnessed it myself.

"Mr. Pope, I'm going to head out and check out P-one, P-two and P-three of the parking garage. Last week we spotted a homeless man who had gotten in somehow and was begging customers for money and trying to open car doors."

"Good idea. Keep me posted," I replied, and looked back down at the shitload of paperwork still waiting for me.

"Man, I hate Mondays," I mumbled to myself.

As a sigh escaped my lips, I realized that I'd better get used to this. Our busiest time of the year was beginning to start. When it got hot, people went crazy. It reminded me of the full-moon syndrome. When there is a full moon, statistics show that the crime rate goes up. I knew from experience that once the temperature goes over ninety degrees, then it's on.

On the other hand, Mia's summer vacation will be starting soon. For three months out of the year, Mia does absolutely nothing. She deserves it, because for the other nine months she's a dedicated, hardworking and caring teacher who makes a difference.

Speaking of Mia, she hasn't said too much about the other night. In fact, she's been unusually quiet. She'll tell me her feelings when she's ready; that's her style. Regardless, I'm so proud of her. She didn't let Brice intimidate her. Back in the day, she pretty much did whatever he told her to. Brice used to take pride in the fact that he kept her in check. On lockdown. Yeah, my baby has come a long way.

And my man Brice . . . well, Brice is Brice. I've known him almost my entire life. He's not going to change; he's still an arrogant muthafucka. But hey, that's my partner, and you gotta love him or hate him.

Three hours later, I had accomplished more work than expected. It had been a productive morning and I'd still have plenty of time to prepare the briefings for my afternoon staff meeting.

I picked up a silver-framed photo of Mia smiling seductively into the camera and wiped a smudge off. Suddenly, line one on my phone rang.

"Christian Pope speaking. How—"

"Hey, hey, save the spiel for someone who wants to hear that shit."

Laughing, I said, "Hey, man, what's up?"

"Kree just called and said she doesn't feel good, cramps or something. So she's not bringing me lunch today."

"Man, you actually have your wife bringing you a hot lunch halfway across town every day?" I asked, shaking my head in utter disbelief.

"Man, she volunteered. I told you, my woman loves to please me, in bed and out. Don't hate; congratulate. Anyway, she doesn't do anything else besides spend my money all day. Lunch is the least she can do."

"Well, you just got it like that, my brotha."

"You damn right. Afterward, I get served dessert, and I don't mean the edible kind."

"That's right; you don't go there. You don't do the downtown route." I laughed, flipping the script on him.

"Man, things change. I've been known to dibble and dabble there a little now. Kree loves it. Drives her out of her mind, man. She'll be squirming and moaning."

"My brotha, you're giving me entirely too much information."

"Come on, you know Mia likes that shit too. They all do."

"Brice, I know you didn't call me to talk about your sex life or mine."

"No, you're right. I didn't. I called to check out your lunch plans."

I glanced down at my watch. It was lunchtime. Damn, where did the morning go? "Nothing in particular. I'll probably grab a tuna sandwich over at Gorin's."

"You can do better than that. Meet me at the Shark Bar in fifteen. It's on me. I need a break."

"Okay, if you insist; I never pass up a free meal. See you in fifteen."

After I arrived a few minutes later at the Shark Bar and was seated at a table over by the window, Christian was still nowhere in sight, and his place of employment was only a couple of blocks up the street. I sat, checked out the gorgeous black women in the place, Georgia peaches, and drank the cup of strong, black coffee I had ordered.

Back when Mia and I were together, she had gotten me into the habit of drinking coffee. Mia would drink cups and cups of black coffee when she was cramming for her exams at State University back in North Carolina. She'd be all tense and stressed. In between her breaks, we'd make love. Sometimes she wouldn't want to, but by the time we were finished, Mia would be all into it, brown legs wrapped tight around my waist, and back arching to receive all of me.

That's the funny thing about sistas: Give them some good lovin', I mean really good, and they'll always come back to you. I'm telling you, set 'em free and they'll come back to you. I know women have those booty-call lists. You know, a ranking of guys who can throw down in the bedroom. Hell, yeah, women are as scandalous as men; they just do their shit on the down-low.

When we were finished, Mia would put on a robe and go back to studying until the wee morning hours. There'd be cups and cups of unfinished coffee sitting around. After Mia left me, I kept the coffee habit. Whenever I drank rich, strong, black coffee, I'd think of Mia and her legs wrapped around my waist, eyes closed, head thrown back in desire.

When I glanced at the front door again, I saw Christian strolling my way. He was dressed in his company's uniform of choice. Dark suit, starched white dress shirt and a conservative pin-striped tie. Christian looked every bit the corporate man. He reminded me of those guys from Will Smith's *Men in Black* movie. As women glanced his way and tried to make eye contact, he strode confidently over my way. Didn't even give 'em a glance.

"Man, I'm sorry I'm a little late. As soon as we hung up, something came up in the parking garage." He pulled out the wooden chair from the table.

"No problem, I haven't been here too long. You got the situation under control?"

"Yeah, we've been having problems with homeless men getting into the parking area and begging for money and harassing the females."

"I'm telling you, man, you could leave that shit all behind and come join me. It'd be like old times again," I said with this *big shit-eating grin* just thinking about the good ol' days.

"Yeah? Well, when would we work? Man, me and you together, we'd never get any work accomplished. Damn."

Christian and I both laughed at that, because we were remembering how buck wild we used to be. Over the years, like all things, our lives had changed.

"Well, how are things going? Are you on schedule with your business plan?" Christian asked as he picked up the menu and glanced down at the lunch specials.

"Pretty much. I've been trying to do most of the physical work the last couple of weeks. Trying to get the carpet laid, buy office furniture, get the phones turned on, stuff like that. Man, I'm trying to do as much as possible myself. You know, save some money."

"Cool. Let me know how I can help out."

"I think one of my old marine buddies might come down from Virginia and come on board."

"Who? Not crazy ass Williams? I know you're not talking about him."

"No, I don't think you ever met Dixon. We hung out in Germany for a minute. He wasn't as wild as your ass, but he's good people. Hard worker."

"Speaking of Germany, did I tell you who I ran into over there? It's a small world after all."

"No, who?"

"That punk ass, Malcolm."

"Malcolm?"

"Man, you know you remember him."

Malcolm was this hotshot marine who tried to get in Mia's pants when we were married. Long story. But bottom line, he tried to fuck my woman, and my woman was going to let him—to get back at me. So I went ballistic on Mia's ass. Put the fear of God in her. End of story.

"What happened?" Christian asked with total interest.

"What do you think? I fucked him up, fucked him up bad."

"Good for you. That bastard deserved whatever he received."

Silence followed as we remembered that time. Didn't want to remember how ugly things got.

As the waiter approached our table with pen and pad in hand, Christian said, "Well, I'm still thinking about your proposition. I just haven't had the opportunity to discuss it with Mia."

"Okay, cool. The offer is still open, man. Always open for you. Personally, I don't see what there is to discuss. Just tell her. Anyway, drop by and check out my place and I can put your ass to work."

Christian and I both ordered sandwiches and iced tea and handed the menus back to our waiter.

"By the way, Kree and I enjoyed ourselves the other night. We must hang out again real soon and, man, I can't wait to meet your daughter. My partner is a daddy. From her photos, she's a beautiful child. Going to break a lot of hearts when she gets older."

"Thanks, Lyric's my heart, and yes, we've definitely got to hang out again. Yeah, the other night turned out better than I thought. We all survived with no major fireworks."

"Mia is still beautiful. I'm sure you are enjoying her as your wife."

Christian didn't say anything, didn't move; he just stared at me with those green eyes.

"What? What did I say?" I asked with obvious confusion on my face.

"Man, you got to cool it with the jokes about Mia."

"Christian, chill, partner. I didn't mean anything by that comment. I mean you two seem happy, very content."

Christian fiddled with his spoon. "We are—very happy."

"Good. I'm happy for you."

"I can't believe you're comfortable with this."

"This what, man?" I asked with raised eyebrows.

"This whole idea that I'm married to Mia, who used to be married to you, who used to beat—"

"Man, I'm cool with it. I admit, at first, I was mad as hell. You know. I felt like she still belonged to me. Felt like I had lost my soul mate. Just the thought of you and her made me see red. I think that was a normal reaction, but now I think we've gotten past all that. You know, let bygones be bygones and look toward the future."

Christian nodded but didn't say anything, just bit into his sandwich.

"Christian, believe me, I'm happy. Our situation is different, but I feel we're adult enough to deal with it. It's evident you and Mia complement each other. I'm cool with that. I was a fool, but, in the end, we both got who and what we wanted. I got a woman who will jump through hoops for me."

He laughed at that. "I hope not. I hope Kree won't jump through hoops. You didn't feel awkward? Not even for a minute the other night?"

I shook my head, but Christian looked at me like I was talking bullshit and burst out laughing.

"Okay, okay, I admit it. It was strange for lack of a better word. In the beginning, it was odd being together again. But like I said before, we're adults and we can handle this. We can make it work."

"I hear ya. You just keep your eyes off my wife's ass," Christian added as he laughed again and took another bite of his sandwich.

"You saw that?"

"Yeah, you damn right." Christian laughed. "That's my woman. Keep your damn eyes off her ass!"

"Well, maybe I did take a peek. Man, I didn't mean any harm, but you know Mia is fine. A brotha still got eyes."

"Okay, okay, enough!" he screamed, faking indignation.

"Changing the subject, Moms told me to tell you that you had better bring your black ass back over to see her. You and Mia. Well, she didn't say the 'black ass' part."

"Sure thing. It was good seeing your moms again. It has been too long, and I've forgotten how Vivica can throw down in the kitchen. Makes me wanna slap somebody," he said lost in thought. "Yeah, I really have missed that."

"'Cause my brotha ain't getting that at home, if my memory serves me right."

"You remember right. Mia still can't cook worth a damn. You wasted your money on that cooking instructor you hired back in North Carolina. I keep hoping and praying that one day a miracle will happen."

We stopped to take more bites of our sandwiches and to get refills on our iced tea. Christian and I were relaxed, enjoying the food, conversation and atmosphere. I noticed the Georgia peaches had finally given up on trying to be seen. They had moved on to bait that was going to bite.

"Man, Kree can throw down in the kitchen and the bedroom. Two of my favorite places. She cooks like somebody's grandmother. She doesn't believe in eating takeout all the time or warming shit up from a can. That night we left your house, before we were out of the car and in our house, Kree was all over me. She helped me out of my clothes. Girl couldn't get enough of me."

"And your complaint? Don't tell me my man can't hang with baby girl. You getting old, man."

"No, no, no . . . Don't *even* go there. Make no mistake; I still have her hollerin' out my name at least three times a week. You know I have to handle my business."

Christian grinned. "Maybe she's faking you out. Women do that shit all the time. Fake the big O."

"Yeah, the BS women who can't handle their business. If they are going to lie there like limp dolls, not move, and fake it, well . . . hell, I don't care. I don't give a damn! I'd rather they tell me they didn't come than fake it and go fuck somebody else. It's not going to hurt my feelings, just makes me work harder."

"Preach now."

I smiled. "I would know if Kree didn't cream anyway. Man, you know. I know I do. I've had enough pussy to last a lifetime. All I know is this: If I don't feel that grip, release, grip, release, that jumpity, bump, bump . . . the way I know it should feel. Then yeah, I'll know she's faking it and don't care."

"True, dat."

"I guarantee—I repeat—I guarantee I can make any woman have an orgasm. My tongue on her clit, two fingers pressed against her G-spot, and boo-yow . . . Guaranteed, my man. Oh, yeah, I got her."

"Kree's a lucky lady."

"You damn right. I have baby girl singing."

"And . . . she has some breasts on her, about a thirty-six-C, big, round, firm . . ."

"Okay, watch it now."

"I have eyes, my brotha," Christian said in a mocking tone.

Lunch continued with laughter, and an old friendship was slowly being rekindled. It felt like I was home again.

Kree

I absently chewed on another fingernail and silently cursed myself for not breaking my annoying habit. I half listened as Mother ranted on and on with so-called advice on how to handle my current situation with Christian and Mia. I made the mistake of mentioning that we would probably go out with them again.

Mother finally took a breath. I started to chew on another nail with the phone balanced on my left shoulder.

"So how does she look?" Moms asked.

"I'm not going to lie. She's a beautiful woman." I wasn't about to tell her that Mia and I shared a more than slight resemblance to each other. I still couldn't believe it myself.

"Yeah, that would make sense. Brice isn't the type of man who would be attracted to a homely, plain Jane."

I murmured something into the phone.

"So?"

"So, what?"

"Tell me more. What happened? How was it?"

"Mother, can't we please talk about something else? How is Miles?" I asked with mild irritation in my voice. I was also mentally picturing what was in the freezer that could be thawed out and cooked for dinner by the time Brice arrived home.

"Girl, we can talk about that irresponsible brother of yours later. Another one of his get-rich schemes has failed. Anyway . . . fill me in."

"God, okay! We talked, listened to music, ate dinner, drank some wine, talked some more and then left. Now are you happy?"

"That's all?"

"Mother, exactly what were you expecting? Nothing really happened. Mia was as uncomfortable as I was."

"What about Brice?" she inquired.

"What about him?"

"Was he checking Mia out? Going out of his way to be near her?"

"No, no, not at all." I didn't dare tell her that I had caught Brice, more than once, with his roving eyes traveling all over her body.

"Well, that's good. How was this Christian person?"

"Oh, Christian was cool. I can see how he and Brice were such great friends."

"Oh, finally some enthusiasm? Did I actually hear some excitement in your voice?"

I didn't even acknowledge that question. I admit, I did like Christian. He seemed very sincere and decent, not to mention fine. Not wasting any time, Mother soon moved on to her next question.

"How did little Miss Mia act?"

"Mother!"

"Girl, shut up and answer my question. I'm trying to get a clear picture here, because obviously you can't see past those rose-colored glasses you're wearing."

"Mia . . . she seemed nervous in the beginning, before her three glasses of wine. She was trying hard to be friendly, but you could tell it was somewhat forced."

"But no passion-filled looks?"

"No, Mother," I said with obvious frustration in my voice now.

"None?"

"It's obvious that Christian and Mia are very much in love with each other. They looked and acted very happy together."

"Well, you met, you saw, you left. So why another get-together?"

"I don't know. That's Brice's friend and we don't know anyone else in the city and—"

"Yeah, that's Brice's friend and, most important, also his ex-wife. Girl, I'm telling you, don't let that—"

"So how's my big brother?"

"Child, that's another hour on the phone. I'll give you the short version. That son of mine has lost over seven thousand dollars to some half-baked business scam, and Vanessa is threatening to leave him."

It wasn't funny, but I kinda chuckled. Miles was forever coming up with some type of get-rich scheme. Even when we were children, he always had a hustle of some sort going. He had big ideas, but they never took off. I had heard that this marriage, marriage number two, was kinda shaky. I guess this was the last straw. I'd give him a call in the next few days. There was a six-year difference between us, but we were still close, as brothers and sisters go.

"Vanessa will forgive him and they'll work it out."

"I hope so for his sake, because she'll take his ass to the cleaners with child-support payments."

Mother and I talked for a while longer about things going on with her, how I was going to start helping Brice out at his office, and we finally ended the conversation with I love yous.

Mia

Time flies, and it was roughly two and a half weeks after our reunion with Brice and Miss Kree. Talk about a blast from the past. That evening was an absolute trip. I still can't believe I actually sat in my living room with my husband, ex-husband and his wife, who looks like a younger version of me, and laughed and talked as if it were the most natural, routine thing in the world to do. I must admit, after an initial awkward moment or two had passed, the self-proclaimed reunion went smoothly.

Brice hadn't changed much in physical appearance. My ex-abuser always took great pride in his body and general appearance. It paid off, because Brice was still as fine as ever, and believe me, he still knows it. As for the rest of the package, I couldn't figure him out. Of course, Brice was on his best behavior for my benefit, because I'm sure Christian had informed him that I was skeptical of the meeting. However, it didn't really matter. I did my part, and Christian was ecstatic, so I was happy. I'd do almost anything for my man.

Kree, on the other hand, was still a mystery to me. I knew it was not a figment of my imagination, but the girl—correction, woman—looked like me. What's up with that? Kree could have been my younger sister. Yeah, she had long hair and was taller, but everything else was me. Christian mentioned he could see a slight resemblance. Yeah, right, there was more than a slight resemblance.

If Kree enjoyed Brice telling her what to do, what not to do, then more power to her. As for me, I'd been there and done that. Never again. Not in this lifetime. That shit about, "Oh, Brice doesn't want me to cut my hair. He likes it long," and then she stared at me. The way I see it, if it's my hair, then I can cut it off as bald as

Michael Jordan if I feel like it. Yeah, the days of a man—namely Brice—controlling me are over.

Other than a few phone calls I answered and quickly handed off to Christian, I hadn't spoken with Brice or Kree since our get-together, and that was fine with me.

Today was a gorgeous, mid-June summer day in Atlanta. The sky was the bluest blue. Everywhere, flowers were in bloom, and the sights and sounds of the city filled my ears.

I love Atlanta! It is such a charming, yet sophisticated, vibrant city. The hub of African American history. I was casually strolling down Peachtree Street, enjoying the scenery. I didn't have to rush home to anyone or anything. Lyric was at Mama's house and Christian was working another twelve-hour shift because one of his employees had called in sick. That's what I love about being a teacher; my summers are my own.

I had just left the fabulous Fox Theater's box office to pick up concert tickets. Jill Scott, Maxwell and a few other artists were performing there in another week, and I wanted to surprise Christian with tickets. He was going to be pleased, because Jill Scott was his girl. And Maxwell was my man! I love to do special things for Christian, and he is always so appreciative.

I was leisurely strolling, stopping now and then to look into a few storefront windows. I wasn't really looking for anything, just enjoying a summer walk. I must have been looking good, because a few businessmen, who probably worked farther down on Peachtree Street, were giving me seriously appreciative looks. I did look kinda sweet with my hot-red halter top, a reddish-orange wraparound skirt that stopped just above my knees, and sexy skin-tone sandals fastened around my ankles. Oh, and let's not forget my red crystal toe ring. I had gotten my hair washed and set the day before at Backstreet Hair Salon. Miss Shirleen had hooked me up. I must admit, I was seriously working it.

I looked up and around, pulled out of my daydreaming when I heard a deep, familiar voice call my name. Standing less than two feet away, decked out in a navy blue business suit and carrying an attaché case, stood Brice, smiling and showing his pearly whites.

Even though it had been a few months since Brice had been discharged from the military, he still maintained a low cut just as Christian did. He looked like he had had a recent edge up and trim. I took Brice in from head to toe before speaking, because I was shocked to see him. I immediately felt uncomfortable being alone with him, even though we were standing in the middle of one of the busiest blocks in Midtown around lunchtime.

Brice spoke first to break the silence.

"Hi, Mia. Imagine running into you. What are you doing down this way?" he asked less than a few inches from my face.

"Hi. I had a few errands to run, but I was just about ready to head home."

We stood there for a few seconds, not sure what to say to each other.

"Have you had lunch yet?" he asked, gently grabbing my elbow to move me out of the way of the lunch-hour pedestrian traffic that was passing by.

"No, I'll probably grab a burger or something on the way home."

"That's not a lunch. Come on, have lunch with me," he stated as more of a command than a question.

"I don't know. I really should be—"

"Oh, come on, Mia. You have to eat anyway, and I don't bite. I know a great Jamaican restaurant not far from here, Bridgetown Grille."

I was still hesitating, trying to think of a way out, but I hadn't said no. I never could say no to Brice.

Before I knew it, Brice's power of persuasion had won me over and we were walking a block over to the restaurant. Along the way, he was excitedly telling me about his plans for his newly formed security firm. I couldn't help but smile at his obvious excitement and his passion for something he truly believed in. Brice always was passionate about his desires.

Brice and I made it to Bridgetown Grille and, as usual during the lunchtime rush, there was a wait of thirty minutes. We somehow managed to grab a seat on a nearby bench as an attractive black couple was being called to their table. Brice and I were seated a little too close for comfort, elbow-to-elbow, chatting about trivial matters to fill in the silent gaps.

When I caught Brice checking out my exposed thigh, my wraparound skirt having parted, I excused myself to the restroom in the far back corner of the restaurant. On the way to the restroom I kept thinking, *The nerve of Brice.* He didn't even try to play it off. For a few seconds I had seen a lustful look in his eyes that I hadn't seen in years. That look always came right before he screwed me like there was no tomorrow.

Once in the restroom, I washed my shaking hands in the sink and wiped my flushed face with a paper towel. I was somewhat composed after that and slowly walked back to the lobby with a smile plastered on my face.

By the time I made it back to the tropical-looking lobby, our names were called. Brice and I followed the tall, dreadlock-wearing waiter to a booth over in the far left corner. There were lit candles on the table, and, as Jamaican music played slowly in the background, a cozy, intimate atmosphere was created. After taking our drink orders of bottled Perrier for me and a bottle of Jamaican beer for Brice, the waiter left us to study our menus for our entrée selections. Brice remembered that appetizers always filled me up too quickly, so we passed on those. He didn't even have to look at the menu. It was obvious that he had been to the restaurant many times. He knew what he wanted. Brice proceeded to give me his recommendations, which consisted of jerk chicken wings, shrimp skewers, Caribbean egg rolls, braised beef oxtail with butter beans, and curried goat.

I used to hate when we were married and he'd order what he thought I would like. Just like a child, I didn't have a say in my meal selection back then. The waiter returned and we made our selections. I purposely didn't order any of Brice's recommendations. He just looked at me. Finally we started to relax and sip our drinks.

Brice spoke first: "It was nice seeing you guys the other week. It was just like old times," he said his eyes never leaving my face.

"Not quite like old times. That's seriously stretching it," I responded in an indignant tone.

Brice picked up on what I was implying. "Mia, you know what I mean. It was good seeing you again. It had been a long time."

"Yeah, I'm glad you could reunite with Christian. You were always like a brother to him, and he missed you." I pretended to be preoccupied with folding my cloth napkin in my lap.

"What about you? Did you miss me, Mia?" Brice asked in a serious, sexy tone.

"What kind of question is that?"

"I think it is a valid one. Did you miss me?" he asked again with his eyes caressing, seducing my face.

I started having flashbacks, started wringing my hands in my napkin, doing anything to get out of answering his question or looking directly at him.

"Mia, can you look at me? Look at me. Is the question really that hard? Did *you* miss me?" he asked in a demanding tone.

I looked up, looked him dead in the eyes, and said, "No, no, Brice, I didn't."

Brice stopped in middrink and laughed. "Damn, that's cold! You're a cold lady, Mia."

At that moment, our waiter, luckily walked over with two steaming plates of mouthwatering dishes.

As we ate our meals, there was more conversation, mostly from Brice.

"How's your food?" he asked.

"It's okay," I said without looking up at him.

"Just okay? See, you should have ordered what I told you to." I did look up at him after that comment. Brice was smiling.

At one point, I had gotten salad dressing on the side of my face, above my mouth. Brice leaned over and started to wipe it off with his fingers, then proceeded to lick it off.

"No, I got it," I shouted, a little too loudly. I quickly picked up the nearest napkin. His touch was bringing back too many memories.

"Here, let me get it. You still don't have it all."

"Brice, stop, I'll do it!"

Brice reclined back in his seat and looked at me with raised eyebrows. "Mia, I thought you were more comfortable and relaxed with me by now. I don't bite, baby. A man can change, you know. Ask my wife. Ask Kree. I touch her with love."

"Brice, it's not even like that. Just don't—"

"Oh, so you *are* comfortable with me? Then why can't you even look me in the eyes when you speak to me? Why is it that every time I'm close to you, you flinch? You think I haven't noticed that? At one point, I knew you better than you knew yourself. Knew you like I know the back of my hand. Why is it that a simple act of wiping food from your mouth makes you freak out? Explain that."

"Why does it matter how I feel about you? It doesn't matter. We are history. End of story. It ended the last time you beat the shit out of me. Remember? Or how soon we forget." I felt my temper rising.

Brice leaned forward in his seat. "I want to make it up to you. I know I hurt you, Mia, and I'm terribly sorry."

"You owe me nothing. You don't have to make anything up to me either. I'm happy with my life the way it is. Christian makes my heart sing—something you were unable to do. I love Christian with all my heart and soul."

"Touché. I know that, and I'm truly happy for you and Christian. He's a good man."

"I know."

Brice nodded his head in amusement, gulped down the last of his beer and signaled the waiter for another.

"Mia, I know you said, with much passion, that you didn't miss me, but I believe you did." Brice looked me over with an arrogant expression and said, "Yeah, I know you did."

"Think whatever you want, Brice; that's your prerogative," I stated nonchalantly.

"Do you want to know how I know?" he boldly asked.

I shrugged my shoulders. "I'm sure you will enlighten me."

"I thought about you a lot over the years, what we had. How good we were together."

"Ummph."

"No, hear me out, Mia. Of course, I couldn't say all this the other evening, but I've missed you. I miss touching your spot and feeling you cream from my touch, from just my hand. I miss feeling and seeing your nipples swell and respond to my tongue and mouth. I miss your warmth when I touched you between your spread legs, and I miss hearing you call out my name so softly like you used to do in the throes of passion. 'Brice, oh, Brice. Oh, baby.' Remember that? Just knowing I was the one giving you all that pleasure . . . Your eyes would glaze over, your legs would start trembling, and I'd know you were there . . . Yes, I miss all that. You were so giving."

I had heard enough! "Brice, I'm outta here. You are a freaking piece of work! You claim to be Christian's friend, but you are such a lying fucker. The nerve of you. I don't want to hear this shit! What is all this BS you're proclaiming? What about Christian? Talk about all the times you beat me down, talk about my black eyes, my bruises, my broken wrist—remember *that*. Well, I can't forget. Talk about that! Yeah, talk about that shit!" I said in a low, menacing voice between clenched teeth. I stood up from the table, ready to book.

"Mia, calm the fuck down! You didn't let me finish," he demanded, roughly grabbing my arm. "See, you are still running from me. Sit down, Mia! Please. As I was saying, I know I did you wrong, very wrong. I'm not proud about that time in my life. You were my woman and I hurt you. Badly. Believe me, I'm happy that you're happy. And I'm very happy with Kree. She's the woman I always needed in my life. Kree knows how to please me."

Brice left the *and you didn't* part hanging in the air, unspoken.

I sat there with a frown on my face and stared at him. I rubbed and massaged my wrist where he had grabbed it. I'd probably have a small bruise.

Shortly afterward lunch ended, and Brice insisted on paying the bill. He refused to take my money. After walking me safely to my car, which he insisted on doing, Brice gently kissed me on my left cheek, right above my lips, before I had the chance to object, and thanked me for having lunch with him. He told me to tell Christian hello and that he would call him soon. But I would never mention this lunch with Brice to Christian.

As I watched him walk away, so arrogant, confident and determined, I realized I was excited. Dampness. Wetness. Throbbing. My nipples, straining against my top, were hard as rocks underneath my halter top. *Damn.* My one weakness had just walked off into the sunset. Trouble had reentered my life. He had already changed my world once.

Christian

Today was like one of those days you see on postcards—picture-perfect. Deep, rich blue sky without a cloud in sight, greenery everywhere the eyes could see, birds chirping in the trees, fragrant flowers in bloom. Kids out riding their bikes and scooters, shouting to each other, having a great time. Just a picture-perfect summer day.

It was a few days after the first of July, roughly a month since the get-together. The Fourth of July had come and gone with no great fanfare. My clan and I decided to rise and shine and attend morning service at Bowler Rock Baptist Church. One of my employees, Joseph Webber, had been inviting me to visit for months now.

Every Sunday, something else always comes up—namely, sleep. I admit, my family definitely needs to do the church thing more often. Most definitely. As it *is* now, once a month is the norm. Most Sunday mornings find Mia and me wrapped up in each other's arms after late-night through early-morning lovemaking sessions.

I know my moms is rolling over in her grave, because when I was growing up, I was in church every Sunday with her, sitting in the front pew. She'd place Randy, my older brother, and me in the first or second pew and would head up to the choir stand. Moms had a beautiful voice, like an angel, and would occasionally lead songs. I used to love to hear her sing. I miss that so much. I miss her. Yeah, those were the days.

However, things change. Events change a person—they change your total philosophy and take on life. And a lot of times, we never see it happening. It's such a gradual change that it becomes a part of our core being without our ever noticing. My moms died; before that, my brother was shot and killed. I felt like God had let me down.

If he could let bad things happen to good people . . . well, there wasn't a need for church and spirituality.

Now, with a family and child of my own and after experiencing and seeing a lot more in my life, I was feeling a strong push to gain back that feeling that church had brought to me in my youth. Peace, serenity and comfort.

Bowler Rock Baptist Church was our site of praise that morning. Service started promptly at eleven A.M. Mia, Lyric and I had a wonderful time. The church flock welcomed us with open arms. We felt genuine warmth and hospitality that morning. Bowler Rock was under the direction and leadership of Reverend Shipler.

Reverend Shipler appeared to be in his mid-forties or so, medium build, clean cut, and the members of the church adored him. The church itself was traditional brick and still had that old-time, Southern-charm feel to it. It hadn't grown too large, too prosperous or too arrogant that the real purpose had been forgotten. That was the problem with many African American churches in the community. With everybody hugging, kissing, smiling and welcoming us, we felt right at home.

That morning, the reverend spoke of the power of prayer. In his thunderous voice, a voice that embodied a spirit wise beyond his years, he spoke of how society had forgotten how to fall down on its knees and pray. When prayers go up, blessings come down. Our parents and grandparents knew the power of prayer. Hell, a lot of us are still around today because somebody prayed for us. Prayed for our well-being and protection.

As I listened to his message, his charismatic bass voice put me into a trancelike state. I glanced around at the congregation responding and holding on to his every word and gesture. There were a lot of amens and hallelujahs being shouted! The beautiful, graceful mothers and the stately deacons, sitting in their special corners, had years of wisdom and knowledge amongst them.

I looked over at Mia in her pretty pink dress, looking like a beautiful angel herself, with Lyric asleep in her lap with a tiny smile on her puckered lips. I realized how truly blessed I was. I had done things, shameful things, in my earlier years. Yet, here I was with a woman for whom I'd die and a daughter who was my heart. I lowered my head and silently thanked God for my many blessings.

Reverend Shipler began to end his message while the choir was softly singing "Stand" in the background. I realized that my prayers regarding Brice had been answered as well. I truly needed—or should I say, wanted—my partner in my life, and it seemed like that was coming together as well. And if I decided to go into business with him . . . Yet, I couldn't get over my uneasiness over the entire situation. I had a nagging feeling about whether I had made the right decision.

After telling Joseph and his family good-bye and how much we enjoyed the service, Mia and I finally made it to the truck, hand in hand, with Lyric sound asleep on my shoulder. Being in a different environment with overstimulation had tired her out. Lyric had been out for the count since church service began. We decided to stop by and say hello to Vivica, Brice's mom. I hadn't been over since that time with Brice, and, according to him, Vivica had been asking about me and requesting that Mia visit as well.

Upon our arrival, laughter and delicious, mouthwatering soul-food smells met us at the front door. We had already seen Brice's Volvo parked out front. Our intentions were to say hello and stay for only a few minutes. We didn't want to intrude. Of course, Vivica was not having that. Before we could even ring the doorbell a second time, Brice answered with a big smile on his face.

He screamed into the house: "Moms, you are not going to believe who the cat just dragged in!" He moved out of the way so that we could enter the small foyer.

By now, Vivica was walking out of the kitchen, wiping her hands on a dish towel hanging from her waistband. "Brice, who's at the door?"

When she got to the doorway and saw us, Vivica was overjoyed, to say the very least. There was so much hugging and kissing going on that you would have thought we had won the Georgia lottery or something. But that's Vivica, a loving, caring, genuine person. She was always like a second mom to me. All my maternal feelings for her rushed back full force.

"Mia, come here, girl, and let me look at you. You look good, baby! Happy! Ohhh, and is this the baby?" Vivica asked as she gently took Lyric from me who was now fully awake and looking around.

Vivica didn't even wait for a response. "Christian, are you sure you didn't spit this child out? God, she's the spitting image of you," she said with a laugh in her voice.

Mia was smiling, but subdued. Occasionally she'd glance over at Brice. Brice was silently standing there, taking it all in. When Mia took my hand in hers, I knew she was uncomfortable.

"Y'all come on in here, and Brice, close that door. I'm so happy to see y'all. Come here; give me another hug!"

It started all over again. When we finally got settled, Vivica took Lyric to an upstairs bedroom to finish her nap. Brice's dad was upstairs napping as well. We found Kree sitting in the living room, flipping through an *Ebony* magazine. Ol' girl barely even acknowledged our presence. No, to be honest, she didn't seem that thrilled to see us, especially Mia. Women are a trip.

"Hi, Kree. What's up, baby girl?" I asked, making my way over to the sofa where she was sitting.

Kree finally put down the magazine, by which she seemed to be so enthralled, and looked up for more than a few seconds. Mia had made her way over to a wing chair as far away from Kree as she could get and pretended to be into the game on the TV.

"Hey, Christian," she said with a sexy smile. "And Mia. Where are you guys coming from or going to all dressed up?" Mia looked Kree's way, but didn't answer her question.

"We just got out of morning church service. We were over at Bowler Rock Baptist Church."

"Me and Brice need to find a church to attend every Sunday. But you know Brice . . ."

Brice took that opportunity to walk back into the den.

"You know Brice what?" he asked out of curiosity. He looked from Kree and then back to me.

Kree looked a bit nervous as she glanced over at Brice.

"I was just telling Christian . . . and Mia that we need to find a church to attend, but you're not big on church."

"Yeah, you got that right. I'm not about to give my hard-earned money to some so-called high-and-mighty preacher so he can buy a larger home or a more expensive car. Hell, no."

Mia was still sitting quietly, watching the game. She didn't even turn around when Brice reentered.

"Mrs. Pope, Mrs. Antisocial, I didn't know you were a sports buff. When did this amazing miracle occur?" Brice asked, moving closer to her and focusing his full attention in her direction.

"I watch sports . . . sometimes. If I didn't, I wouldn't spend any time with my husband during baseball, football or basketball seasons. There are many things you don't know about me." She crossed and then uncrossed her silky legs.

Brice still made her uncomfortable, and sometimes I thought my man got amusement out of doing so. Not that he did it intentionally. Their history together—our history together—made it uncomfortable for Mia. I felt that, in time, it would pass, though.

"Well, Kree knows to stay out of my way when sports are on. She doesn't know a damn thing about any of the games, and her silly-ass questions drive me crazy. It gets on my damn nerves. I don't have time to explain every play. She's around for the halftime entertainment."

Brice glanced in Kree's direction and she gave him this look—this evil as hell look.

"Isn't that right, baby?"

"Yeah, that's right. Excuse me, I'm going to see if Mama Vivica needs any help in the kitchen." Kree hurried out. When she passed Brice, he playfully slapped her on the ass. She threw him that evil look again, but Brice just laughed.

"Did I miss something? No, man, just forget Kree. Don't pay her any attention. She's PMS-ing, tripping or something. We had an argument earlier and she's still pissed. She'll get over it," Brice said without any concern in his voice.

Mia turned and looked at him. A few minutes later, she excused herself to go check on Lyric upstairs.

"You'd better chill, man. You ran the women away. I told you about those crazy-ass male-chauvinist statements."

"Yeah, whatever! They'll both get over it, and if not . . ."

Brice retrieved the remote from the mahogany coffee table. He turned up the volume, flopped down on the sofa, and, before you knew it, Brice and I sat back and enjoyed the rest of the game on the tube. Vivica brought in some iced tea and we were in heaven until dinnertime.

Brice

The game was just about ending when Moms called us to the dinner table. That was cool, because the game wasn't even close; the Atlanta Braves blew the Cincinnati Reds away. I smiled a big shit-eating grin as I retrieved my twenty dollars from Christian and made a big, dramatic display of placing it in my wallet. I couldn't help but boast that he shouldn't bet with a pro; I knew my sports.

Moms was like, "Wash your hands and come and eat," as if we were little children or something. Anyway, the smells coming from the kitchen were getting to me. Tantalizing smells. My stomach was growling, flip-flopping, and doing all sorts of shit. I loved to eat my moms's cooking. She could throw down in the kitchen. Kree was a pretty good cook, but she couldn't touch my moms. Close, but no trophy.

I'd heard them earlier, Kree, Mia and Moms, in the kitchen talking back and forth. I couldn't make out what had been said, but it sounded like Moms was doing most of the talking. I'm sure that was an interesting conversation, very interesting. I wish I had been a fly on the wall. It was kinda funny, actually. I don't think I've ever had two women together, knowingly, with whom I've been intimate. That, by itself, was a trip.

I was glad Kree's mood had improved, because I was sick and tired of her bad attitude when she couldn't get her way. I give her an inch, she wants two inches more. I had finally agreed to let her work in the business with me . . . on a part-time basis, because she was supposedly so bored at home.

This way, Kree could leave work around one o'clock or so every day and have my dinner ready by the time I arrived home. I did need help with some of the administrative and office tasks. Kree was good at stuff like that. She even came in and gave the place a woman's touch with the plants and framed artwork she had purchased. Real homey and warm.

However, that isn't good enough for baby girl. Kree wants to work full-time. Hell, no! Hell to the no! Now she was pissed and silently sulking. And she had better silently sulk; she knows better than to keep riding me about it. I don't play that shit, and she definitely knows that.

Dinnertime was cool! Just like I thought, Moms threw down. She really outdid herself. We sat down to a baked ham, crunchy fried chicken, seasoned collard greens, fried creamed corn, black-eyed peas, mouthwatering corn bread, potato custard and iced tea. This was her typical Sunday meal.

My pops, when he was younger and healthier, had a hearty, robust appetite. So back in the day, he expected a real soul-food meal on Sundays, usually right after church service. Moms never gave up the habit. She still cooks as if she's cooking for an army of people on Sundays. Leftovers are given to a few of the elderly who live on their block. Sometimes, the pastor and his wife come over and have dinner after church service.

We all gathered in the formal dining room, around the mahogany table, held hands, bowed our heads, and Moms led us in a quick prayer to bless the food she had prepared. She also gave thanks that we were all together, as family. That's what's important to her; that we come together as family. The ladies had brought all the food in from the kitchen, placed it on the table, and we sat down to a hearty feast and lively conversation.

Kree and myself sat on the right side of the table with Mia and Brice directly across from us. Moms was seated at the head of the table. Pops's spot was painfully vacant. Moms didn't want to wake him, since he was sleeping soundly.

Pops was still having very restless and fretful nights. Wednesday, I had plans to accompany Moms to visit his doctor to find out what was really going on with him. As it is, I don't know my old man anymore. He's a shell of the man I used to know and sometimes feared. At times, I don't think he even recognizes me. That's the tragedy of his disease.

At first, all you could hear was the sound of forks and spoons clanking on plates as dishes were being passed around and everyone began to dig in. Moms had this huge smile on her face, like this was the ideal scene for her.

"So, Kree, Brice tells me that you work with him for part of the day now." Everyone's attention focused on Kree.

"Yes, Mama Vivica. I've been doing it for a couple of weeks now, and it's working out okay. It gives me time to make it home and get dinner cooked by the time Brice walks through the door," she answered in between bites.

"That's good. You said you were getting bored sitting around at home all the time. I know what you mean; it can get old real fast."

Kree shook her head in agreement and looked out the corner of her eye at me.

"And what about you, Mia? What have you been up to for your summer break?" Moms asked to bring Mia into the conversation.

"Not much of anything, to be truthful. On the days when Lyric doesn't go over to Mama's house, we hang out at the park or Chuck E. Cheese's or just do whatever. Christian works such crazy hours, so he's never home."

"I remember those days well. I used to look forward to my summers. Sometimes I would take classes at Georgia State to keep abreast of things, but most of the time I played homemaker, wife and referee. Brice and Christian were always up to something or another." Her eyes glazed over and she laughed at the memory.

"Moms, me and Christian weren't that bad!"

"Yeah, right, my memory hasn't left yet. Y'all were always into some mess, usually involving some girl or girls."

Kree and Mia just looked at each other knowingly and smiled. Actually, it was one of the first genuine smiles I'd seen Kree direct at Mia. I don't know what Moms talked to them about earlier in the kitchen, but it had made an impact. The ice-princess persona Kree

directed toward Mia was slowly but surely melting. I saw Mia catch
my eye and look quickly down into her lap.

"Moms, you're right, Brice was always dragging me into some
scheme or another. I was always an innocent bystander who got
caught up and sucked in. I'd end up taking the fall with him."

"Yeah, right. Tell that lie to someone who believes you."

Everybody laughed at that because they knew better. Needless to
say, Christian's and my reputations preceded us in the local community. Older men and women in the neighborhood still remembered
and told tales about our adventures—or should I say misadventures.

"Kree, if you have some free time some evenings or weekends, I'll
be happy to show you around to some of the stores where there are
some good buys." Mia reached for the flowered bowl of fried corn.

"Okay. Sure. Brice is not big on shopping, so he is no help. Cool.
I'll let you know."

"Girl, let me tell you. There's a T.J.Maxx over on Industrial
Boulevard that has some great buys. New inventory comes in on
Wednesdays. Great deals, gorgeous stuff and designer labels."

From that point on, the conversation flowed freely, and second
helpings and dessert were consumed without hesitation. By the time
Moms brought out coffee, we were all sitting around like stuffed
pigs, too full to move. All I could think of was chillin' on the sofa for
a good hour or two. However, I was too lazy to move. Christian was
reclining back like it would take a miracle to pry him out of his
chair as well.

The women started to clear the table and help Moms wash and
put up the dishes. She wouldn't let them wash the dishes by themselves. Moms claimed she knew where everything went, so she
might as well help. After Christian checked on Lyric and brought
her downstairs with him, her tiny arms wrapped around his neck,
we chilled in the living room, watching some Clint Eastwood Western on TV. I should say that Christian was watching it. I was getting
my nap on more than anything else. Ten minutes later, I was in full
sleep mode.

Mia and I had gotten the kitchen back in order, with the dishes washed and dried, the leftovers securely covered in aluminum foil on top of the stove, and the floor swept clean. Mama Vivica kept a neat, spotless kitchen. She had finally retired upstairs with a plate for her husband. She was going to try to see if she could get him to eat something.

Even though Mama Vivica is retired, I don't know how she does everything she does around that household. The lady, at her age, is a bundle of pure energy. Never sitting down to relax, always going, going, going, and, according to Brice, his Pops was taking more and more time and energy to take care of. This concerns him because he didn't want his moms to become a prisoner in her own home. It's obvious that Mama Vivica loves her husband and will do whatever it takes to make him comfortable.

Mama Vivica gave Mia and me strict orders to relax, sit down, rest and mostly talk. She wanted us to *talk*. She had already filled Tupperware bowls with food for us to take home for Monday's meal and probably enough for Tuesday's as well.

When Mia and I walked into the living room, the first thing we saw was Brice knocked out on the sofa. He had the nerve to be slightly snoring. Christian was dozing on the love seat with his head bobbing back and forth and his mouth slightly open. Lyric was the only one up and about, with the remote in her tiny hand, channel surfing. We laughed at our so-called big, strong men knocked out for the count. I know my husband. Good food and good sex always put him to sleep.

Mia and I decided not to wake them and let them rest, because they both have been working really hard the last few weeks. Our men are good providers! Mia picked up Lyric, whose tiny hands were already outstretched for her mommy, and we went back into the kitchen for another cup of coffee and a snack for Lyric. While Lyric ate a little bit of our previous meal, Mia and I got acquainted.

I'm not going to lie and say I instantly liked her, but I will say that I allowed myself the opportunity to get to know her better. Yes, it was tense at first. I realized I had treated her like nothing because I had all these preconceived notions about her.

Mia didn't appear to be the woman who was going to steal my man, as Mother would have me believe. In fact, Mia's a lot like me. Yeah, as much as I hate to admit it, we are a lot alike in many ways. A black woman trying to make it in this world of ours. Loving our men too much. Compromising to meet their needs and keep them happy. Juggling families and careers. Struggling to keep our identities intact and giving, giving, giving. Sometimes to everybody but ourselves.

So Mia and I sat there with cups of black coffee between us and reintroduced ourselves to each other. We found out we have more in common than not. One major similarity is our love of Denzel Washington. We both have undying love and devotion to this godlike man. We agreed we'd leave our husbands for him and never look back. When Mia informed me that there was a Denzel Washington marathon at a movie theater across town, we both agreed that we simply had to go. By the time we woke up our husbands, it was a done deal!

Mia

Vivica's little talk worked wonders. When I first walked in her house, I instantly felt uncomfortable and out of place. I felt I had made a terrible mistake by dropping in, and then when Kree treated me so coldly, as usual, I was certain it was a mistake—major. Vivica knew all my dirty laundry with Brice, and I felt ashamed even though he was the one beating *my* ass. Brice treated me like nothing and I treated him like everything.

Years earlier, when Brice and I were still married, an incident happened at Vivica's house in the guest bedroom upstairs. Vivica walked in on Brice beating my ass over some trivial stuff. Let me see . . . Oh, yeah, Brice didn't like what I was wearing that day. He had straddled me on the bed and I was crying my eyes out, begging him to leave me alone. He was beating the shit out of me with his fist, and Vivica had to pull him off of me. I had a black eye, bruises and not an ounce of dignity left to show for it.

That was the evening Vivica confessed to me that her husband, Brice's father, had beaten her, and Brice had grown up exposed to that. I felt a closeness to her. She has always been nice and sweet to me; Vivica is just that type of person. But that evening, I felt a bond, a oneness. Like we belonged to a secret sorority or something. The Battered, Beaten, and Bruised Club.

After my divorce from Brice, I guess I divorced the entire family. It was easier that way. I hadn't talked to or seen Vivica since. Today, it all came flashing back, hitting me in the face when I stepped through her front door. Not much had changed about the house, and standing and grinning right in my face was *him*.

Vivica must have sensed my discomfort, because when I came

downstairs after checking on Lyric, she called me into the kitchen to chat. I slowly walked in and had a seat at the table. Kree immediately made up some half-assed lie and excused herself to another room. I couldn't stand her ass.

"Don't mind Kree. You know she's intimidated by you. You scare her," Vivica said matter-of-factly, with a shrug.

"No, I don't know what her problem is. Kree doesn't say two words to me at one time. I haven't done anything to her." Anger was in my tone.

"Yes, you have. You were married to her husband. A husband that she adores."

"Believe me, she can have that shit," I barked before I thought about Vivica being the shit's mother.

"I'm sorry, Vivica," I said sincerely.

"Baby, I know this is hard for you and it's just as hard for Kree. Understand, you are both making huge sacrifices for your men's happiness. That's very admirable."

I nodded in agreement and thought about what Vivica was saying. It was true.

"Mia, I never forgot you over the years. In fact, I thought about you often. I had come to love you like a daughter, and you were the first woman that my son truly loved. I would often ask people who knew your family about you. I knew exactly when you and Christian had that baby. I even stopped by the hospital to see her in the nursery."

"Did you?" I asked in amazement.

"Yes, baby, I did. Mia, I never condoned what my son did to you, and I regret to this day that I didn't speak up and tell you to get out before it was too late. Love doesn't conquer all! I was living your life every day with his father, so I guess I wasn't in the right frame of mind myself to dish out any advice."

"Vivica, I never blamed you for what your son did to me. That was his choice."

"I know that, baby. I just wish I could have done more. I wish I could have been brave enough to tell you to leave him, but I wasn't even brave enough to do the same thing myself with Brice's father."

We stared at each other for a few precious minutes. Vivica looked down and wiped her hands on the blue-and-yellow dish cloth with pictures of ducks tucked in her apron.

"I don't know how much that child in there knows about all this. Knowing my son, she probably doesn't know much of anything. My son tends to keep his women in the dark. However, I know she loves him just like you did."

"I did love him."

"I know you did, baby."

"But now I'm in love with Christian so much. Christian is my lifeline." A huge smiled crossed my face.

"I know. And like I told Christian, I'm happy for you. You and he both deserve happiness in your life. That man in there has gone through so much in his lifetime. Losing his brother and his mother. Never knowing his father. I was so pleased that Christian found you. I sincerely mean that."

"Thank you. You don't know how much that means coming from you." I stood to give her a hug.

"I pray every day that my son has changed, that he has learned from his mistakes with you. I pray for that each and every day. Brice has a second chance at happiness with Kree. Do you realize how rare it is to find true love twice in a lifetime?"

At that moment, Kree strutted back through the kitchen without a backward glance.

"Kree, come here, child," Vivica said. "Sit down."

Kree looked from Vivica to me and back to Vivica with bewilderment on her face.

"Kree, I know this is hard for you, this entire, uh, situation you ladies have placed yourselves in. However, you and Mia are going to work out your differences today."

"Vivica!" I shouted in shock.

"No, I mean it. You and she could be blood sisters, you look so much alike, and I'm not going to have it. You both have more in common than you think. Walking around each other not speaking. Well, I'm not having it. Life is too short to waste it on negativity.

You both made this compromise for your husbands. Well, look around. They're happy as larks and they're going to be together come hell or high water. They have that bond."

There was complete silence. I was looking down at the light blue tiled floor like it held the secret to life, while Kree was chewing on her thumbnail. Vivica continued.

"The two of you can be unhappy for the rest of your lives or learn to get along. At least be civil to each other. Can you do that?"

Kree and I both looked down at our hands.

"Kree, you are the worst. Mia doesn't want your man. Remember, she divorced my son, not the other way around. Mia, do you want Brice?"

"Hell . . . I mean, no, ma'am."

"That's what I thought. Don't you see the way she dotes on Christian and that adorable little girl asleep upstairs?

"Kree, you are young. I know you don't have family here, and I love you, baby, like a daughter. I feel like I can talk to you like this. Besides, at this point in life, I'm too old to care."

"Mama Vivica, I—"

"Hush, child, I know. Both of you, try to get along. Why please your husbands and be unhappy in the process?

"And Kree, start standing up to that man more. Don't get me wrong—I love my son dearly—but don't let him walk all over you, baby. Quit letting him tell you what to do and what not to do. Stand up to him sometimes."

Kree opened her mouth to say something, but then I guess she changed her mind, because nothing came out. She just continued to chew on that one pitiful-looking nail.

"You need to talk to Mia. There are two sides to every story."

Kree and I both looked at each other as Vivica walked out the kitchen.

The last thing she said was, "Talk."

Later that day, after dinner, we did just that.

Christian

"I'm sorry, baby. Yeah, I know it's the second time this week. Yeah, yeah. I know. I'm sorry. I'll make it up to you and Lyric. I promise." I had as much disappointment in my voice as I heard in Mia's on the phone.

"You got that right, Boo. You will make it up too, so don't work too hard. You'll need all your strength. I'll wait up for you," Mia said in a naughty voice.

"No, baby, as much as I'd love to see your beautiful, smiling face when I walk in the door, go to sleep. I don't know what time I'll make it in tonight."

"Okay, if you're sure. Love you."

"Love you more. Talk to you later." I slowly hung up the phone and put my head in my hands.

I was working a double shift once again. Summertime was always a hectic time at my job, but I was also two men short. I had terminated one fellow who wasn't working out, and another associate was taking a paternity leave because his wife had just had their first child. Tonight Mia and I had plans to go out to dinner. However, those plans were out the door now. Duty called.

I was feeling really bad because Mia and I hadn't done a lot of family-togetherness things since the summer had begun. My mother-in-law had agreed to keep Lyric for the night while Mia and I went to a quiet, romantic dinner at a new restaurant in Midtown I had wanted to check out; some of the men at work couldn't stop talking about it. After a few drinks, I was going to go home and make love to my beautiful wife until the sun rose.

Sex was usually a three- to four-time-a-week event at my house.

Lately our lovemaking sessions were down to *nada* because I was usually exhausted when I walked through the door. After a quick shower and dinner, no matter how much desire and passion was there, I was out for the count.

Tonight was going to be special. I missed the feel of my wife's sexy body beneath mine. A perfect fit. I missed looking down and seeing her stare silently into my eyes with a deep, yearning desire for me. I missed the heat and passion of our kisses, the swell of her breasts as I kissed her neck, and her sweet moans when I first entered her wetness. Mia makes me feel wanted, desired and needed. Mia makes me feel like a man.

I couldn't get her off my mind, so I picked up the phone to call her back. She picked up on the second ring.

"Hello?"

"Listen, baby. I'm sorry about tonight. I hate disappointing you and I miss you already."

"Boo, it's not a problem. We'll have many more evenings to go to dinner. You are so sweet! My li'l sweetie pie. Listen, I have Sharon holding on the other line."

"Oh, I won't hold you then. Tell her I said hello and y'all don't gossip for too long."

"Ha ha ha, so funny, Boo. We don't gossip. She just got back in town from visiting her parents, so we have a lot of catching up to do. She's going to pick up a large pepperoni pizza and come over."

"Well, good. Have fun. I feel better now because I know you'll be entertained for a while. Bye, baby—I'll talk to you later."

"Bye. Love ya, Boo." She hung up the phone, still laughing.

Yeah, I did feel better now! I could focus on the tasks at hand. I successfully completed some paperwork without too many distractions and even managed to finalize the schedule for the following week. I posted it on the bulletin board along with other informational documents. As I did a quick scan of the monitors, my mind replayed last Sunday evening.

I'm not sure what Vivica said to Mia and Kree, but it worked wonders. Miracles actually. No, they are not the best of friends and, due to the circumstances, will probably never be, but at least they were civil to each other afterward and Kree wasn't directing the majority of her conversations in my direction, excluding Mia.

Mia and Kree actually carried on full-length conversations and ogled and goggled over Denzel Washington's looks, acting skills, his walk and then back to his looks. Personally, I don't see the attraction. And no, I'm not hatin' on my man.

Before we left Vivica's that evening, our ladies informed us that we were taking them to this Denzel Washington—or Denzie, as they referred to him—marathon. Brice and I had no choice but to agree. We were still stunned that Mia and Kree were communicating with each other and tried to determine what had happened to change things between them.

Vivica volunteered to keep Lyric for a couple of hours, since she and the baby had taken a liking to each other. Mia and I rushed home to change into something more casual and planned to meet back up with Brice and Kree at their condo before heading over to the show.

Everything was cool and flowed smoothly! Our ladies were sexy-cool in their jeans, halter tops and open-toe sandals, both of them with painted toenails and anklets. Not knowing any better, anyone would think they were sisters. We all chatted casually on the ride over, which was about a twenty-minute drive. Brice drove, so Mia and I were sitting in the backseat of his Volvo. Kree was all over Brice as usual; you couldn't tell where he began and she ended.

When we arrived at the movie theater, we bought popcorn with extra butter, sodas, Raisinets, Gummi Bears, the works. Mia has a habit of scattering Raisinets in her popcorn. At first, I thought it was weird, but now I like it that way myself. Mia's like that; she has a way of rubbing off on you. Before you know it, you've adopted her ways.

A few minutes before the show started, we were seated with the ladies in the middle.

Mia and Kree were like two teenage girls the way they carried on over Denzel. It was almost disgusting. In fact, the way most of the women were carrying on was pitiful. I, for one, was not impressed. Overall, we had a really good time. After the movies were over, we played the arcade games in the lobby, like school-age kids. Brice and Mia were even getting along with each other.

At one point we spotted a Pac-Man game in the far corner by the wall near the exit door.

"Oh, my God, Brice, look at that. Pac-Man." Mia pointed and quickly walked in that direction.

We all kinda did a double take, because this was the first time since our reunion that I had heard Mia direct any comments in Brice's direction.

We followed behind Mia and were all standing around the game.

"Remember when we used to go to that arcade in Fayetteville on the weekends and I'd *destroy* you in Pac-Man?" Mia said with obvious glee in her voice as she glanced back at Brice.

"Yeah, I do remember that arcade. It was called All-American or something like that," Brice said.

"Yeah, that was it. And they sold some of the best hot dogs and cheese pizza."

"However, I don't recall you destroying me in Pac-Man, Mrs. Pope." Brice came up behind Mia.

"Kree, girl, you'd better come over here and feel your husband's forehead, because I think he has a fever and is delirious or something." Mia glanced over at Kree and me, now seated on a bench near the game watching their antics.

"Oh, it's like that?" Brice questioned.

"Yeah, buddy. You know I used to kick butt, namely yours. You couldn't touch me and you hated it. You hated to lose!"

"That sounds like Brice—always a sore loser," Kree kidded back.

"Okay, prove it then. Show me. Show Kree and Christian that you can back up your words. Put up or shut up."

Mia turned around with her hands on her hips, hand held out, and looked at me. "Baby, give me fifty cents so I can show Brice who's the man."

I dug into my pocket and handed Mia four quarters. As spectators, Kree and I soon lost interest. This was obviously between Mia and Brice. We started chatting about her working at Brice's company and how she was enjoying that.

The more I talked to her, I realized there was something very feminine and sexy about Kree. I'd be looking at her when she talked and she'd blush, push a strand of her hair out of her face, place it behind her ear and lick her full lips. The air-conditioning in the place was cranked up to freezing. Kree's nipples were standing at full alert when I glanced down at them a couple of times. I couldn't help but notice, because she had the prettiest pair of breasts. Kree was actually kinda shy, and I guess my being so close to her made her nervous.

My initial impressions of her were wrong too; baby girl did have a mind of her own that came out when she wasn't around Brice. She was also very intelligent. Kree told me about some of the musicals that were coming to the Fox Theater in the fall. If Brice didn't take her, she planned to go by herself. For some reason, I believed her. She had a passion for dance.

When I glanced up again, Mia and Brice were still playing the game with much laughter. I did my second double take of the day. Brice was standing behind Mia, bending down, with his arms on both sides of her and his hands on the Pac-Man machine maneuvering the gears. With Mia standing in between his arms, they looked intimate, like a couple. Mia laughed at something Brice said and leaned back, for a brief second, into him.

She glanced in my direction with this look on her face—this gleeful, nostalgic look. I smiled. She smiled back.

Kree remained silent by my side. Brice didn't look at her. Kree managed to give me a strained smile.

Finally Mia turned around. "Kree, come over here and help your man lose with some dignity. Like I said, he's no match for me." Brice laughed his hearty laugh and threw up his hands in defeat.

"Yeah, come here, baby. Let me touch that sexy ass of yours and maybe it'll bring me some good luck."

Kree walked over and they exchanged places. How symbolic.

I've grown in my admiration of Mia. Really, I can't get her off my mind. For the longest time, I grieved over the termination of our marriage. I felt like someone close to me had died. I loved that woman to death and a part of me will probably always love her. Even though I treated her wrong, dead wrong, I still felt that Mia had betrayed me by divorcing me and not giving our marriage, our love, another chance. I went from loving her to hating her. I wanted to do some serious bodily harm to her at one point. Then I met Kree, and Mia was moved to another part of my heart. To the back, in the corner. At least, that's what I thought.

Last Sunday I saw a glimpse of the old Mia, the Mia whose heart hadn't frozen in regard to me. I saw a glimpse of the Mia who was passionate, fun-loving, giving, and loved me dearly. I tried to play it cool, but I started having flashbacks. Pieces and fragments of our life together kept passing before me, playing out in my mind. Mostly the good times, the passionate times, the times when Mia was totally un-inhibited with me. I used to love that about her. Back then, she'd do almost anything I told her to. And when she leaned back into me, at the Pac-Man machine, I got an instant hard-on. Mia always had that effect on me. There's always one who can take you there with no effort.

To be honest, I'm proud of her! Mia is following her dreams and is good at what she does. Christian told me she was teacher of the year at her school last year. I can't lie—she has matured into an even lovelier woman, and wife, than when we were together. Mia has this confidence about her—something, I'm sad to say, I stifled when we were married. I kick myself every day for what I lost in her. I'm happy for and jealous of Christian all at the same time, but that will forever remain my secret—the jealousy part, anyway.

After we dropped Mia and Christian off at their car, we made plans to have dinner at our house the following Wednesday. We realized that they had never visited us before. That night, Kree and I had some of the best sex we've had in a long time. Kree was singing. It was off the chain! Later that night, I had the weirdest dream. It was so vivid that I thought it was real until Kree woke me up. She said I was calling out something and tossing and turning.

In the dream, I was making love to Kree. I was on top, going in and out slowly, and she was looking deep into my eyes with her big innocent eyes. I pulled her face to mine for a kiss and when I opened my eyes again, Mia is staring up at me with this look of pure ecstasy while I grind inside of her. She was crying softly. I asked her why she was crying, because I thought I was hurting her. She said, "I've waited so long."

I shook my head, looked back down, and then I was on my knees and I was doing it from behind her. I reached around to caress her face with my hand; she put my finger in her mouth and slowly sucked on it for a few seconds. As I pulled her head back by her hair to kiss her neck, I looked and it was Kree again and she was crying. Kree asked, "How can you do this to me? Why? All I did was love you."

That was the dream. I was going back and forth fucking Kree and then Mia. Finally, I couldn't tell one from the other, they became one, and just when I was explosively coming and shouting out, Kree woke me up. I'm not even going to try to figure that one out.

The dinner Wednesday was pleasant enough. It was pretty laid-back and casual. Kree took an exorbitant amount of time planning the meal. I'm like, "It's only Mia and Christian, baby. We aren't entertaining the king and queen of England." But that's my Kree; everything had to be perfect. She finally decided on a garden salad with red-wine vinaigrette dressing, baked salmon with rice pilaf, and

steamed long-stemmed green beans, and, for dessert, we had strawberry shortcake. Kree even brought out our good china.

I knew Kree would be a little pissed at me because I arrived late.
Dinner was at six o'clock, and I showed up from work at six thirty.
To top it off, earlier, I wasted so much time on a document that I had
to rewrite twice. And I had a ton of phone calls to place and return.
I can't get some of the kinks out of my software; it's just not running
smoothly. Kree is not big on installing computer software, and I'm
definitely not. I hate the thought of hiring someone to set me up
when everything is almost working. They will charge me an arm
and a leg for a couple of hours of work. All of this put me behind
schedule.

Anyhow, when I walked through the door at six thirty, the first
and only person I saw was Mia. She was standing in the middle of
my living room wearing this sexy, knee-length, wraparound red dress
that tied at the waist, with sling-back red shoes, flaming red toenail
polish, and bright red lipstick. She even had her short hair gelled
down on the sides. Needless to say, Mia took my breath away. Talk
about sexy, totally hot and sensual.

I slowly closed the door and turned away from her in order to
give myself a few seconds to compose myself.

"I apologize for being so late. Where is everybody?"

"Your wife ran to the corner store for rolls or something, and my
husband is in the restroom."

I noticed the way Mia always referred to Kree and Christian as
"your wife" and "my husband."

"Oh, I see. By the way, you look lovely. You always did look great
in red. And something smells wonderful in the kitchen. I'm starving." I loosened my tie and hung up my suit jacket in the coat closet.
I never hung up my jacket; I'd usually toss it on the sofa for Kree to
take care of.

"Oh, yeah, Kree should be right back. She wouldn't let me help
her with anything. She seemed right at home in the kitchen."

"Yeah, she's a great cook."

"I'm glad. I know that's important to you."

There was a silence. We just stood there smiling at each other. I took a step forward and Mia took one step back.

"Oh, I was looking for something to put in the CD player."

"Here, let me help you." I slowly walked over to her.

"Don't we have déjà vu going on here?" Mia joked.

"Ummm, you smell good. Good enough to eat."

Mia gave a nervous, high-pitched laugh, the one she used to do when she was uncomfortable, and turned back around to focus on the CDs.

I knew she was embarrassed at the thought of me eating her out.

"What do you have on?" I asked, walking up behind her. Mia turned suddenly around and we were looking at each other, eye-to-eye. Her breasts accidentally rubbed up against my chest. She gasped like she had been burned, and jumped back from me. I grabbed her arm to keep her from falling. Man, when my hand touched her bare flesh, I felt an electric shock. Seriously. It was my turn to let go.

Christian walked into the room at that moment. "Man, you'd better get your ass in there and change before your wife gets back from the store, because she is already pissed that you're late."

"You ain't never lied. Okay, y'all make yourselves at home. My home is your home, *mi casa es su casa* and all that jazz."

Mia was rubbing her arms, her back turned to Christian. I heard Kree at the front door, fumbling with her keys, before I saw her. By the time Kree arrived home with fresh baked rolls in hand from the local deli, I had showered and dressed in khaki pants, a tan shirt, and loafers. We were sitting in the living room listening to the Alicia Keys CD, talking about how talented she was and how she was going to be a superstar, and sipping on chilled chardonnay.

"Hey, baby." I got up to help her with the package and to give her a wet kiss. Her mouth was hot and wet and yearning for more when I pulled slowly away. Out of the corner of my eye, I saw Mia watching us intensely. When I looked in her direction, she dropped her eyes to the floor.

I didn't want a damn attitude from Kree for the rest of the night because I was a little late. So I figured I'd pour the lovey-dovey on. Just as I thought, Kree forgot all about my being late. I'm telling you, most women just want to be babied and pampered and they'll melt in your mouth. Ha ha ha.

I've been with a lot of women, all ages, races and ethnic backgrounds, in my lifetime, and they're basically all the same. Some are just a greater drain on your wallet than others; they need more from you. They require more maintenance. But believe me, when the loving is good, they are all the same in bed; they come like cottage cheese.

In no time at all, Kree was calling us to the dining room. The table setting looked great along with the delicious food. Once again Kree had outdone herself. To create an atmosphere, she dimmed the lights and adorned our crystal candleholders with some gold-trimmed white candles. With Alicia Keys playing in the background, we couldn't ask for more other than good conversation. Christian and Mia fixed their plates, at Kree's request, and dug in after I told them not to wait for us. After Kree fixed my plate, she finally sat down to dinner as well.

I noticed the look Mia gave Kree. When we were married, Mia used to hate with a passion to fix my plate. We would have major, major arguments about it. I remember one time I broke every plate in the damn house, because if I didn't eat then no one would. Mia felt that if I was a grown man with the use of both hands, then I should do it myself. I told her that she was my wife and that was a form of respect, something a woman should do for her man. Take care of him and all. It would almost kill her if I made her fix my plate if we were out in public at a buffet-style restaurant.

"Brice, how's business, man?" Christian asked.

"Man, didn't I tell you? I got my first two clients the other day. Nothing major, just some security work at this upcoming rap/hip-hop venue."

"That's great. Looks like you're in the house."

Christian raised his wineglass for a toast. Everyone followed suit. "To much success and prosperity."

Everyone chimed in. "Cheers."

"But that's why I've really got to get my software problem solved, and soon."

"Mia's pretty good at stuff like that. Baby, why don't you go over and take a look at it?" Christian asked, looking in my direction.

"Uh, sure," Mia responded hesitantly. "I can drop by one day next week and take Kree shopping afterward."

The remainder of dinner was pleasant. We talked about all sorts of things, as friends do. I caught up on my ex-mother-in-law, heard all about the joys and tribulations of teaching these new generation kids, and learned about the newest adorable thing Lyric was doing. Based on Mia's comments, it was also obvious that Mia wasn't pleased with the long hours Christian was putting in at work. Kree was making plans for us to attend some of the ballets that were coming to town. I'd have to think about that. Ballet wasn't my thing.

Christian and Mia finally called it a night around nine thirty, because Christian had to work the next morning. All in all, it was a good evening. We had all come a long way.

Kree

"**S**ure, Mother. Just let us know when and where and we'll pick you up at the airport. Hartsfield-Jackson." Mother had informed me that she wanted to pay us a visit soon. Real soon. Secretly, I was dreading it, because she and Brice didn't get along for more than five minutes at a time, and it wasn't a good time anyway. I didn't need more drama.

"Are you sure you're feeling better, baby? You might have that bug that's going around. You're not usually this quiet."

"Yes, Mother. I'm feeling a lot better than I was earlier this morning. I just needed a day off from work, a day to myself."

"Good. You take care of yourself down there. Don't let that husband of yours run you ragged, girl."

"Mother, he doesn't run me." I felt my temper rising.

"Yeah, that's what you say. I see otherwise. You wouldn't know the truth if it slapped you in the face. Anyhow, I'm just glad you finally got that little ex-wife problem resolved. It's not kosher to have a relationship with your husband's ex-wife. And how does his best friend end up marrying his ex, anyway? It doesn't make sense."

I said yes and no a few times for effect and let Mother go on and on. I had lied and told her that we hadn't seen Mia and Christian in a while. I would have never heard the last of it if she knew we were all hanging out a lot lately. It had been about a week since I last saw them. Today was a sick day for me, or at least a sick-of-Brice day.

"Okay, I'm going to hang up now and give your brother a call at work. Take care, baby, and I'll talk to you soon. Go get back in bed and drink some orange juice. Don't you even think of preparing that man's dinner today. Let him fend for himself for a change."

"Mother, that man's name is Brice."

"Yeah, whatever."

"Okay, Mother. I gotta go. Bye. I love you," I said before we started to argue.

"Love you too."

It was almost noon and I hadn't even dressed yet. I had heard Mother leaving a message on our answering machine and had instinctively picked up without even thinking about her long lectures. Still not in a hurry to shower and dress, I sat down on the sofa, turned on the TV and flipped through a few channels. Nothing caught my eye, just a lot of talk and court shows. I didn't need more drama in my life, even if it was somebody else's. Yesterday, I'd experienced more than enough drama to last me for a lifetime. It all started out so innocently . . .

I was in the kitchen finishing up our dinner dishes while Brice sat at the kitchen table, reading the sports page in the *Atlanta Journal-Constitution.*

"Brice, what's wrong, baby? You've been distracted lately," I asked him with concern etched in my voice. I know my husband, and he had been too restless the last few days and nights. Something was up; something wasn't right with him.

"Kree, for the fifth time this week, I'm fine!"

"Sweetie, I was only asking because—"

"Well, don't ask. Damn it, can you understand the words coming out my mouth?" he asked, glaring over at me.

"I was only concerned, thinking—"

Brice jumped up from the table, his face an angry mask. "Don't think! Goddammit, how many times do I have to tell you to stay out of my muthafuckin' business? You got that, Kree? Is that simple enough for you? Leave me the fuck alone. You—you're my damn problem! Always fifty questions."

"Fine!" I screamed as I ran by him and threw the wet dish rag in his face.

"Kree, get your ass back in here. Now!" he screamed at the top of his voice.

"No, leave me alone," I cried from our bedroom.

"I'm not telling you again, Kree!"

"No!"

When I glanced up again Brice was towering above me with his face scrunched up in a total fit of rage and his fists clenching and un-clenching at his sides. Before I could get over the surprise and react, Brice yanked me up from the bed by my hair and dragged me back into the dining area. I was crying, kicking and pleading the entire way. When he got to the spot where the dish rag lay, he stopped.

"Now, pick it up and place it neatly in the sink," he said calmly, pushing my face near the floor.

I didn't move. The only sound was my cries for him to stop. It was chilling because Brice was so calm and cold.

"This is my final request. Pick it up or you're going to regret it in exactly five seconds. One, two, three . . ."

I reached down and quickly picked up the dish cloth before he reached five.

"Good girl."

Brice, still holding me by the hair, led me over to the sink. I placed it neatly in the sink as he requested. He let go of my hair with a smirk on his face. Brice pushed me away like discarded garbage.

I ran back down the hallway. "*I . . . hate . . . you!* I hate your ass so much! You make me sick! I can't stand your damn ass," I screamed in between hysterical sobs and clenched teeth.

"What? What did you say to me?" he yelled. He caught me by the arm and readied his fist to strike me.

"Repeat that shit to my face. I'm waiting, Kree."

By now, I was hugging the wall in fear and trying to get as far away from him as I could. Brice was out of control.

"You promised—you promised, Brice . . . that you'd never hit me. You promised," I sobbed. My body gave out and I slunk down to the floor in a squatting, fetal position.

Something broke in him. He came to his senses. His entire de-meanor changed in an instant. His seething anger changed to instant regret.

"Kree, I'm not going to hit you. See, you're doing that same shit Mia used to do all the time. Provoking me. Come here." He pulled me up into his strong arms.

"I'm sorry, baby. I love you, Kree." He kissed me all over my face and neck, over and over again.

I couldn't even look at him. I looked down at the floor. He cradled my chin in his hand and forced me to look up into his light brown eyes.

"I love you, Kree."

"Okay."

"Did you hear what I said?" he asked with just a hint of anger in his voice again.

I knew what he wanted to hear.

"I love you too," I chanted with little to no emotion.

Shortly afterward, I took a quick shower and put on the ugliest nightgown I owned, the one with the big flowers that buttoned up to my neck, and went to bed. I got as far over on my side as I could without falling out of the bed. Brice was still watching TV or something in the living room. I hoped his ass fell asleep and stayed out there all night.

I couldn't sleep even if I wanted to. I lay under our crisp sheets and thought crazy thoughts concerning our marriage. I heard Brice when he came in and got ready for bed. My body instantly tensed up. After he had stripped down to his boxers, Brice got under the covers. I was hoping—praying actually—that he didn't try to force me to have sex with him. So I remained perfectly still and pretended to be asleep. I even threw in a few soft snores for good measure.

I could feel him glaring at me even though my face was turned away from him. I held my breath and prayed silently. If he wanted some and I didn't give him any, then there would be hell for me to pay.

At one point, Brice pulled the sheet off of me. My ugly granny gown was hitched up around my thighs. He was sitting with his back against the bedpost. I could feel his eyes boring into me, taking in my body inch by inch. I felt so vulnerable that I wanted to yank the sheet back over me.

"Kree, I know you aren't asleep."

I didn't say anything. I didn't move an inch. I didn't breathe.

"Okay, you can play possum if you want to."

I closed my eyes tighter when he bent down, reached around me, pulled my gown up further, pulled my silk panties to the side and stuck his fingers in—two, then three—and moved them around slowly. In and out. Playing with me. He used his free hand to open my legs wider.

"Don't worry, baby. I don't want any tonight." He withdrew his fingers, caressed my right breast through my gown, and squeezed a little too hard.

I flinched as Brice placed his hand under my gown, pulled it up far enough to expose my chest, and began to play with my nipples for a few moments in between stroking and squeezing my breasts.

"I love you so much, Kree, and I hate when you make me treat you like this. Good night," he whispered in my right ear. He withdrew his tongue from my ear and palmed my buttocks. "Sleep tight."

Mia

"Sharon, I don't know. I can't explain it; I'm not sure what happened myself. Maybe it was the talk Vivica had with me and Kree or just being in her house again. But I faced my demons, and Brice isn't the monster from my past anymore." I balanced the phone on my ear as I painted my nails.

"Um-huh."

"Um-huh. What the hell is that supposed to mean?" I paused in midstroke of applying Passionate Red nail polish.

"Girl, you still have feelings for him?"

"Hell, no. Sharon, you must be out of your damn mind. How could you even . . . Hell, no. Girl, have you forgotten all that drama I told you about him?"

"Girlfriend, you were married to the man for almost three years, but I can see how being around him is bringing back memories."

"Yeah, you're right, bad ones."

"True, but you admitted that there were a lot of good ones as well. And that the man was so good in bed that you still have flashbacks," Sharon added with humor.

"Well, whenever I remember that, two seconds later I also remember his fist meeting my face."

"Well, personally, I don't think it's such a good . . ."

"Go on. Don't hold back now. Tell me."

"Nothing, just be careful, Mia. I don't want to see you hurt again, nor big-head Christian." She laughed.

"I'm a big girl, Mama Sharon."

"Speaking of big heads—where *is* Christian?"

"Where do you think? Working as usual. I rarely see him anymore. Only coming and going."

"Girl, don't complain. At least he has a J-O-B and is gainfully employed. You ought to be glad you have a dependable, hardworking man who provides for his family. You know he'd do anything for you and Lyric."

"I know. I just get lonely around here. Lyric is usually fast asleep by eight o'clock every night, and then I'm here by my lonesome." I sighed into the phone and blew on my nails to dry them faster.

"Well, it's all part of his job. He is the head of security. Get yourself a puppy or a cat. Take up a hobby. Learn to entertain yourself. It's all about self-love, girlfriend."

"Ha ha ha. Why don't you come over for a while and keep me company?"

"Sorry, can't do. It's my oil-lube night. You know I just got back from visiting my parents, and I'm craving some now. Craving it."

"Oh, you'd take a man over your best girlfriend?" I asked, joking.

"Hell, yes! Tonight, anyway. You got a warm body with a dick attached to lie down with every night. Christian gives you yours whenever you want it. All you have to do is roll over."

We both laughed.

"I'm about as needy as you are. Sex has been virtually nonexistent in this household lately."

"Well, you and Christian got to work that out. I can't help you there."

"I hope not!"

"Me, I've got an hour to get ready before the maintenance man pays me a visit. Tall, dark and bald-headed. Just like I like 'em."

"You are stupid, girl. Stupid."

"Whatever. Talk to you later, dear."

"Okay, if you have to go."

"Yeah, I have to go. Mia, talk to your hubby and tell him how you feel."

"Maybe."

"Girl, you need to quit holding everything inside. It's not good for you. You told me how you feel—tell him. The last I heard, he doesn't bite."

"Yeah, you're right, Oprah Junior. I will. Have fun tonight."

"You know I will. I'll call you tomorrow and give you all the juicy details," she said with a devilish laugh.

"Bye, I'll talk with you later."

"Bye."

As soon as I hung up the phone, it rang again. I thought it might be Christian calling, so I grabbed it on the second ring.

"Hello, sweetie. I have a surprise for you tonight."

"Well, hello to you beautiful," I heard Brice say, laughing. "Mia, I think you have me confused; this is Brice."

"Yeah, I think I do too. I thought you were Christian," I said, visibly embarrassed.

"Other than your plans for later tonight, what's up, lady? What's going on?" Brice asked, teasing me.

"Nothing much."

"I take it Christian's not home yet."

"No, he's not. Christian is working, as usual. He's at his second home."

"Why do you sound so down, Mia? Oh, I remember—you could never stand being alone, could you?"

"Is it that obvious?"

"Yes, it is. Do you always answer a question with a question?"

"Yes, the ones I don't want to answer."

"Touché."

"Where's Kree?"

"She'd better have her ass at home." He laughed.

"So where are you?"

"Oh, I'm not home yet. I'm calling from my office, getting ready to leave in about another ten minutes."

"I see Christian isn't the only one who's a workaholic," I said with dismay.

"You caught me, Mia," he replied with mock indignation. "Can't hide anything from you. Yes, I have a great love for shelter and food and clothing. It's true. Can't fool you."

"You are so wrong for that." I started to laugh. I heard Brice laughing too, which made me laugh all over again like he had said the funniest thing in the world.

"Mia, it's good to hear you laugh," Brice said with total sincerity in his voice.

I didn't say anything. Brice took that as his cue to continue on. I listened.

"I'm serious. I'm not sure what happened recently, but I'm thankful that you don't hate me anymore."

"Hate you? I never hated you, Brice. Even after everything you put me through, I never hated you. Far from it."

"Well, that's good to know. All these years, I thought the opposite. I am curious, though. What changed things over at Moms's?"

"I don't know. I really don't. I've asked myself the same question. Vivica's talk, being in that house again, Kree's acknowledging me, my love for Christian. It all came together to make me forgive you, I guess."

"You don't know how long I've waited to hear you say those words to me . . . that you forgive me. Because believe it or not, just because I didn't love you the way you wanted me to doesn't mean that I didn't love you with everything I had, Mia. Know that."

"I know. I know, Brice," I whispered into the phone.

There was a silence that lasted for a few seconds, a release and letting go of past wrongs. I heard Brice sigh. I exhaled.

"Well, my beautiful Mrs. Pope, I'm going to let you go. It's been a real pleasure talking to you this evening. I mean that. Tell that husband of yours that I called and that we need to talk about my proposal. He'll know what I'm talking about."

"Okay, I will. For the rest of the week, he should be here in the evenings. However, I'm keeping my fingers crossed. I'll believe that when I see it."

"You do that. And Mia, thanks again. By the way, I've been practicing my Pac-Man skills and I'm ready to take you on again." There was much laughter in his voice. "When are you coming down to check out my computer software?"

"When do you need me?"

"Yesterday."

"Yesterday. You sound like you're in dire need of my skills."

"You know it. You couldn't begin to know how much."

"Okay, let's do this. I can drop by tomorrow around eleven thirty or so, and then afterward Kree and I can go out for a late lunch and go shopping or something."

"Cool."

"Tomorrow it is then. Let Kree know."

"Yeah, tomorrow it is. Good night, Mia. Sleep tight."

"Good night, Brice." I gently hung up the phone with a genuine smile on my face. It was still early, so I poured myself a glass of wine, put on some soft jazz, curled up on the sofa and chilled by myself. Sharon would be proud.

Much later I was awakened by a soft caress against my right cheek and light butterfly kisses. I moaned and opened my eyes slightly to find Christian smiling down at me with his eyes full of lust, desire and love. Christian gently lifted me up, carried me to our bedroom and tenderly placed me on our bed. He undressed me down to my lacy red bra and panties and made a trail of kisses from my face down to my toes.

When he came back up, he stopped at my thighs, massaging them, and opened my legs wider. The last thing I remember was how sexy he looked, his shirt wide-open, revealing his toned stomach. He whispered that he wanted to make me feel good, make me happy. I felt his warm breath down there. He blew a few times. I closed my eyes and tilted my head back. Christian kissed my stomach and he told me to relax. I felt his fingers inside me. "Relax, baby, and let me take you there." After that, I had a taste of heaven as I sang a melodic, seductive love song and he drove me to ecstasy.

★ ★ ★

The next morning, I got up, whistling a tune, and fixed breakfast for Lyric and myself. We ate waffles, Lyric's favorite, with bacon and eggs. After we were both bathed and dressed, I called Mama to see if she could keep Lyric for a few hours. I had promised to check out the computer software for Brice to see what the problem was.

"Mama, hey. I'm glad I caught you in."

"Hey, baby. I decided not to go down to the senior-citizens' center today. I wanna can these beans that Sister Laura brought by yesterday. There're fresh from her garden. Should give me about six jars or more."

"She always looks out for you. Listen, Mama, I need a favor. Can you keep Lyric for a few hours?"

"Child, that's not a favor. You know I love spending time with my favorite grandchild."

I laughed. "She's your only grandchild."

"Bring her on by. Where are you running off to this early? You're usually still sleeping your life away at this time of the morning."

"I promised Brice that I'd take a look at his computer."

"Since when are you going out of your way to accommodate that man, to use the term 'man' loosely?"

"Mama, I'm not going out of my way. I'm off for the summer and I have nothing better to do with my time today. I'm just helping him out."

"Where's your husband?"

"Working."

"Does he know you're going down there?"

"Yes, he does. In fact, he suggested that I take a look at it." I thought back to last night. His oral skills turned me out. Christian wouldn't let me move or do anything. He told me to just lie there and enjoy. He got pleasure out of seeing me come—several times. Needless to say, I was feeling too good this morning.

"Okay, you're going to let that man seduce you right back into his open arms."

"Mama, be for real. First, you tell me to see Brice to put closure on that time in my life, and now you're telling me to run before he snares me. Make up your mind."

"I didn't tell you to become his best friend. I've seen firsthand the effect that man has on you. Makes you act irrational. Foolish."

"Let's drop this. Okay? Before we both say something we shouldn't. I love you, Mama, and I know you're only looking out for my best interests, but I'm not that person from a few years ago. Brice is not going to make me do anything I don't want to do."

"I hope not," I heard her whisper more to herself than to me.

"It's ten thirty now; we'll be there shortly."

"Okay, sweet pea. Drive carefully. See ya soon."

I smiled because that was my childhood nickname. When I was growing up, my daddy and Uncle Larry used to call me that. Said I was sweet as a pea. They were both deceased now. Not a day went by that I didn't think of them. I missed them so.

After dropping Lyric off at Mama's house, I headed over to Brice's company, Security Unlimited, Inc. I had a vague idea where it was located. I had driven by with Christian before and he had pointed it out. After turning around for the second time and going back near West Peachtree Street, I soon found it a block over. I parked on the street, locked the car door, walked a block up and went into his dream.

I was impressed! I don't know what I was expecting, but it was tight. I mean, they had done a lot with the place in a very short time. There were potted and hanging plants everywhere and framed prints on the brightly painted walls. There was a warm, vibrant, inviting, homey feel to his place; like I said, I was impressed.

When I walked in, Kree looked up from the receptionist/waiting area and actually smiled at me. She was filling out some type of paperwork.

"Hi."

"Hi, Mia. I hope you didn't have too much trouble finding us."

"No, no problem at all. I was only turned around for a few minutes. I hope your husband told you I was dropping by to take a look at his PC and to take you out to lunch and shopping if you're free."

"Yeah, he did, about thirty minutes ago."

"Men," I said as I shook my head.

"Yeah, men. Anyway, he's back there; go right in, second office on the left." Kree pointed behind her. With her thick hair pinned up and a nice pantsuit on, Kree looked very professional and efficient.

I walked past a storage closet, a restroom and two other doors and found Brice in the larger office, with his crisp white shirtsleeves rolled up, talking on the phone. I knocked on the partially open door, and he motioned to me with his free hand.

"Your woman just walked in. Yeah, she found us okay. You wanna speak with her? Okay. Hold on."

Brice handed me the phone, reclined in his rolling chair and scrutinized me closely while I talked to my husband. I could feel him taking in my body inch by inch, but this time it didn't make me nervous. This time it made me feel sensual and sexy as I ran my fingers through my short hair. In my jeans, midriff T-shirt and tennis shoes, I felt sexy-cool.

"Hey, Boo."

"Hey to you. I see you made it okay. How're you feeling today?" Christian asked with a hint of devilment in his voice.

"I feel great," I exclaimed, glancing over at Brice, who wasn't even pretending to ignore my conversation.

Christian and I both laughed at our private joke because he knew I couldn't talk freely.

"This morning you were sleeping so peacefully that I didn't dare wake you." I'd usually get up with Christian and go back to bed after he left for work. I loved spending those early-morning minutes with him during the summer. It was always so peaceful and reaffirming. I'd walk him to the door and give him a deep, passionate kiss to get him through the day.

"Well, it was a late night, but well worth it."

"You got that right. Can't wait to have a repeat. Listen, I'll let you get to work. I'll talk to you later, baby."

"Bye, sweetie, love ya." I handed the phone back to Brice.

He retrieved the phone and kinda gave me this look—a look I couldn't quite read. He got up, gave me his chair and proceeded to point out and walk me through the problems he was experiencing on his PC. I'm no computer expert, but I know a little sumthin'-sumthin'. It appeared that some of his software hadn't loaded properly and had to be reloaded. I set up his AOL e-mail account, gave him our e-mail address, at his request, and helped him to organize a few files into folders.

That was it. By then it was around two thirty or so. The morning flew by. Kree apologized and gave me a rain check on the lunch and shopping. She had to rush home to prepare Brice's dinner.

I thought Brice was going to tell Kree that she could go shopping with me and not worry about his dinner. He didn't say a damn word. I got the distinct feeling Brice didn't want us to get too chummy. Understandable. I could tell her an earful, and Kree and I could definitely compare notes. I thought how lucky I was that Brice was no longer my problem. I shook my head in disbelief and walked out the front door behind Kree. Amazing.

My feelings flipped back and forth. Just when I was beginning to like him as a friend, he'd do something foul or make some crazy-ass comment. In the days and weeks that followed, I'd discover that would become our pattern. A love-hate relationship.

The summer was quickly zooming by and I was cherishing each sunny day. I had gotten into a routine of sleeping in, spending quality time with Christian when he wasn't working, visiting Mama and Sharon, and taking Lyric to the park, the zoo and the neighborhood playground. Boring, but routine.

About two weeks after I had gone to Security Unlimited, Inc., Christian and I went dancing with Kree and Brice at Club Kaya in Midtown.

We had a ball and Kree showed out. The girl had mad dance skills. It's a shame that Kree isn't using her talent in some artistic capacity. The more I'm around her, the more her true personality revealed itself. Kree wasn't as shallow as I initially thought. Brice overshadows her with his dominant personality and she dulls in comparison.

We had been at the club for about two hours. I had one too many drinks, but I was so thrilled to be out of my house, interacting with other adults, that I went all out. I had a nice little buzz going, feeling real good. I knew Christian wasn't going to let anything happen to me. Not his sweetie. So it was all good. Besides, he was enjoying all my touchy-feely moves on him and reaping the benefits. Alcohol makes me horny as hell.

There was lots of laughter and drinking going on. Kree and Christian danced together several times as did Brice and me. I made sure it wasn't on any slow songs.

At some point, Kree and Christian were hanging out on the dance floor again. She was all over my man, but it didn't make me jealous. My Boo only had eyes for me. Being a woman, I still kept a watchful eye in their direction just to be safe. Kree isn't that innocent if she's married to Brice. I know the demands he makes in bed. Anyway, that left Brice and me alone together at our table in the far corner. We had decided to sit that one out. Mistake. That was when the weird shit began. *Twilight Zone* shit. *X-Files* shit.

Brice stared at me with a look of amusement on his face as he nursed his rum and coke.

"What?" I asked, giggling like a schoolgirl.

"Don't you think you've had enough? You know how you act when you drink. Drinking has always gotten you into trouble, Mia."

"This is only my second—no, third—screwdriver," I slurred as I tried to focus on him through slitted eyes. "What are you talking about? Anyway, you're not my dictator anymore. So you can't tell me what to do. Now," I crooned into his face. I was up-close and personal. Did I fail to mention that drinking also makes me flirt? We were so close we could have kissed. I felt his warm breath, saw his long eyelashes, and could feel the heat rising off his muscular body.

"I'm crushed—your dictator? Mia, I wasn't that bad. Cut me some slack."

"Oh, yeah, believe me, trust me, you were. That's how it felt, anyway. Always telling me what to do, what not to do, and how to act. And if I did something you didn't like, well, we both know how I suffered the consequences." The alcohol made me talk freely. We were eyeball-to-eyeball.

Brice continued to sip on his drink and watch me intensely. He leaned back in his seat and sized me up.

"Do you do that shit to Kree? Or was I just the lucky one?" I touched his knee with my hand.

"See what I mean? You talk that crazy bullshit when you get a couple of drinks in you."

"Tell me, Brice, do you hit her, too? I've wanted to know from day one." I was on a roll. "I haven't seen any bruises."

"No, Mia, I don't hit Kree. I have no reason to. She knows how to be a woman and how to treat her man," Brice said, scoring a point.

"And I don't?" I asked in hurt and disbelief.

"Back then, you weren't the woman I wanted you to be." He touched my right hand, which was resting on the table. I felt an instant shiver traveling up my arm.

"Yeah, right, barefoot, pregnant and in the kitchen was your ideal woman. And, oh, let's not forget sucking your dick." I moved my hand from within his reach. I didn't want him to see the effect his touch had on me.

"I had no complaints about the latter. You did that one really well," he exclaimed with a smirk.

My eyes shot daggers his way. There was a long silence. I redirected my attention back to the dance floor. I was determined not to let Brice get to me. Not this time. I bopped my head and snapped my fingers to the hip-hop music. People watched and checked out my man on the dance floor. He looked gorgeous dressed from head to toe in black.

"Mia, did Christian tell you I saw your old friend over in Germany?" Brice said matter-of-factly.

He got my attention again. I turned my head away from the dance floor to glare at him.

"Who? My friend? I don't know anyone in Germany."

"Oh, yes, you do. Think. He remembered you all too well. Had wonderful memories."

"He? Now, I don't know who you're talking about."

"Yeah, you do. Think real hard . . . I ran into your old friend Malcolm."

I felt a cold chill as I looked into Brice's piercing stare. I nervously picked up my glass and gulped. Yeah, I remembered Malcolm all right. Tall, dark, bald-headed, fine. Sexy as hell. Full lips. And he quickly turned into my worst freaking nightmare.

"Remember Malcolm? Remember he was the private who was eating my ex-wife's stuff and getting her all hot and bothered in our house on our sofa?" he said calmly with an angry glare in his eyes.

I didn't answer. I was having flashbacks to those times when I saw that look, and remembered what would follow: his open hand making contact with my body. However, I couldn't turn away from Brice; I was too scared, and his eyes were hypnotic.

"And what did my beautiful ex-wife do? She let him taste her and enjoyed it, from what he told me. Said you were eager and asking for more. Couldn't get enough."

I still didn't say anything. I was frozen like a deer caught in approaching headlights.

"Don't you want to know what happened?" Brice asked as he leaned forward.

I slowly shook my head. I never took my eyes off him.

"No? Well, let me brief you anyway. First, I made him tell me exactly what happened between you and him. Then I proceeded to beat his muthafuckin' ass, sent his punk ass to the hospital, and dared him to tell anyone I had fucked him up. Nobody messes with my woman.

"So, sweetheart," he said, gently taking my glass from my trembling hand, "my point is that I really hate to see you drink too much because you do stuff that you shouldn't. Don't you agree?"

I nodded in agreement and Brice smiled knowingly.

"Are you enjoying yourself? By the way, you look beautiful to-night. That red dress is doing you much justice."

"Thank you," I managed to murmur in my alcohol-induced confusion.

What the hell? It was like the previous conversation never took place. His mood changed back to party mode in just that instant. He was like Dr. Jeckyll and Mr. Hyde. Brice was playing chaos with my emotions and he knew it.

"Let's dance." Brice firmly took my hand and led me to the crowded dance floor, on the opposite end from Christian and Kree, with no room for my refusal. As soon as we started to get into the upbeat tempo, it ended and the deejay flipped it and put on a slow jam. I tried to walk away from the dance floor, but Brice grabbed my hand and pulled me back to him.

"Come on, Mia, dance with me. I don't bite. What are you afraid of? Huh? It's only a dance. Just a dance, Mia."

I looked into his sexy eyes as he placed my hands slowly around his waist and pulled me closer. I felt his solid mass . . . I remembered *us.* I instantly felt hot.

"Just one dance," Brice said again, holding up a finger.

From that moment on, every nerve ending in my body was on high alert. I felt every touch of his strong hands as they pressed against me, just barely caressing my exposed back. His warm breath tickled my ear when he leaned into me. I felt his muscles ripple as I cautiously slid my hands up his strong back. My nipples responded to his touch and pressed into his shirt. Brice's cologne was intoxicating, and, for a moment, I closed my eyes and breathed in his smell. I used to yearn for that smell. *Manly.* I felt his strong hands slowly descending down my back toward my butt.

I opened my eyes. I pulled away to protest.

"Shhh. Close your eyes. Relax," Brice whispered so softly that I wasn't sure if I imagined it or not.

Brice pulled me back to him and I felt it, hard, thick and pressing into me. I was flushed and instantly wet.

The song crooned on. I couldn't see Christian on the other side of the room. So I knew he couldn't see us.

By now, my nipples were straining against the fabric of my halter dress, and when Brice palmed my butt with his hands and pressed me into his groin, I lost it. I let out an orgasmic, soft moan. Realizing my reaction, I jerked away from him and quickly pushed my way through the crowded dance floor to our table before he could stop me.

When Brice, Christian and Kree finally returned to our table a few minutes later, Brice was laughing and telling them about some dude in the club who couldn't get a dance if he paid for one. Brice didn't even look in my direction as he continued his story. I grabbed Christian's hand and laid my head on his shoulder.

I whispered, "Are you ready to go, Boo? I'm kinda tired. I wanna go to bed, feel your warm body next to mine and just snuggle."

"I can't think of a better way to end the evening." He kissed me on the tip of my nose and pulled me closer.

"You're shivering. Are you okay?"

"I'm fine now that you're here." Absently, I rubbed his back over and over. Christian's presence was always calming and soothing to me.

A few minutes later, Christian and I said our good-byes and were headed out the exit door. As I glanced back, the last thing I saw was Brice kissing Kree on her neck and Kree laughing at something Brice said while he stroked her hair away from her heated face. I turned away with my body still humming from his touch.

A couple more weeks came and went and it was almost August. Where had the summer gone? Christian was back in work mode and I had made my displeasure obvious in my own way. I simply wouldn't speak to him besides one-word answers. Christian would get mad, which was rare, and ask me why I couldn't express my feelings to him. Doors would slam, we'd sleep in the same bed without touching, and he'd accuse me of not trusting him, not sharing with

him completely, and holding back my love for him. These were ac-
cusations that had been tossed around by Christian throughout our
marriage. And then he would do something fantastic or say something funny, and the whole episode of not speaking would pass over
like a mild summer's rain.

We hadn't seen Kree and Brice since the night at the club. However, I had talked to Brice on the phone on a couple of occasions
and everything was cool. I had thought about that night long and
hard, and I think it was the alcohol and my active imagination reading too much into things. Brice was a true flirt and was just messing
with me that night. In our brief conversations, he certainly hadn't
mentioned the incident or said anything out of line to me. So I
didn't mention it to Christian, and life went on. I did say to Christian that I thought Kree had a crush on him and that I was keeping
an eye on them. He laughed; I didn't.

So another Friday night found me sitting at home . . . alone.
Christian was pulling a double shift for some reason. To be honest, I
didn't even hear the explanation because I was so pissed. Lyric was
over at Mama's for the night, and Sharon had a date—maintenance
time. So we couldn't even hang out. When I came in that evening
after dropping Lyric off, I poured myself some of the white wine we
had left in the fridge, lit some aromatherapy candles, turned on some
light jazz, pulled off my sandals and planned to spend a productive
evening working on my personal computer that was sitting on the
kitchen table. Christian had brought it in from our guest room.
Mama had recruited me to put together a senior-citizen's directory
for her center, and I had been putting it off for much too long.

I was pretty mellow after my third glass of white wine and had
actually gotten a lot accomplished on the spreadsheet. I was startled
by the doorbell ringing. I glanced at my watch and realized it was already nine P.M. I wasn't expecting anyone. I peeked through the
peephole and was surprised to see Brice standing there. I opened the
door to his bright smile.

"Hi, Brice."

"Hi. How are you?"

"I'm fine, but Christian isn't here. Sorry. He's pulling a double shift at his second home."

"Damn. Well, my bad. I guess I should have called first."

We were still casually standing in the doorway. Brice gave me the once-over.

"You look nice tonight, Mia. Are you going somewhere?" he asked, inspecting my black halter top that scooped down low in the front and my wraparound miniskirt that showed off my sexy legs.

"No, it's just me and my computer tonight. Exciting, huh?"

"Listen, can I use your bathroom?" His eyes searched inside the living room, which was dim.

"Sure, come on in." I opened the door wider for him to enter and stepped aside. "You know where it is. Help yourself."

Brice nodded and strolled to the bathroom. I closed the front door and walked back to my computer. When Brice returned, I was busy sorting the spreadsheet in alphabetical order.

"You seem to be hard at work on something." He walked over behind me and looked down at the computer screen.

"Yeah, I'm trying to finish this up for Mama so she can quit bugging me." I laughed and looked up at him.

"Cool. Maybe you can show me a few tricks on Excel since you seem to be the expert. Compared to me, anybody is an expert, though."

"Yeah, if you'd like." I really wasn't in a hurry for him to leave because I wanted the company. He was right about one thing: I hate being alone.

I began to show Brice the basics and explain the functions of the different icons on the spreadsheet. Suddenly Brice interrupted me.

He was still standing behind me, sipping a glass of wine, to which he had boldly helped himself. "Mia, you smell so good, girl. What do you have on?" he asked as he playfully sniffed my neck.

For some reason, I realized how close Brice was to me and that we were very much alone.

I laughed, "You always ask that. I'm wearing Seduction."

"Seduction, huh?"

"You got it. Remember the name so you can buy it for Kree." I glanced back up at him.

"How did Kree suddenly get into this conversation?" he inquired with annoyance in his voice.

I just shrugged it off. I really wasn't up to getting into a confrontation with Brice.

"You know you can sit down," I said, slowly kneading my neck with my left hand to get rid of some of my sudden tension and strain.

"No, I'm fine. I like standing. Go on with your lecture, Miss Schoolteacher; I'm listening," he laughed.

I continued on, and, now and then, I would rub my neck.

At some point, I felt Brice's warm hands firmly on my shoulders and he began to massage them in vigorous strokes.

"What are you doing?" I pulled away from his hold as if I had touched fire.

"Chill, Mia. You look like you need a good massage, that's all. You look tense, so I'm helping you out. I have magic fingers, you know."

"Oh, do you now?" I asked, feeling that I would give in to him.

"Relax," he cooed, "let me ease some of your tension."

Finally, I leaned back into his masculine hands and closed my eyes for a second. It did feel wonderful.

"Does that feel good?" he whispered seductively into my ear.

"Yes, yes, it does. You missed your calling." The man did have magical fingers. I relaxed and enjoyed his touch. The CD started to replay as I reached for my wineglass to take another sip. I was rather mellow.

Gradually, Brice's massage was becoming erotically and sensually charged.

"Here, let me untie your top so that I can massage your back easier." Brice began to untie the knot without my consent.

I quickly jumped away from his prying fingers.

"What are you doing?"

"Relax, Mia, just hold the front of your top. I promise I won't peek. It's not like I haven't seen your breasts up-close and personal before."

I hesitated for a moment and leaned back. I slowly relaxed again and closed my eyes. I felt his strong hands making their way to the edges of my breasts. Barely touching them. Teasing them. I didn't say anything. I was stunned. Again, I spoke no words when Brice bent down and started to lightly kiss the back of my neck, featherlight kisses. I felt shivers and my body started humming again.

"Relax, baby. Let me make you feel good like I used to. Remember? Don't you want that? Trust me," he softly whispered in my ear as he slowly pulled my top away to expose my breasts. "Beautiful."

"Wait, what about . . . ?" I asked anxiously. "I can't do this. I can't. No, stop, Brice!"

"Shhh. Shhh. Calm down! This is just between you and me, baby. I don't want to hurt Christian or Kree either." His voice was calm like he was talking to a child.

"But I can't hurt . . ."

"Relax. This is just about you and me. At this moment, no one else matters. Trust me; they never have to know. Never. This is our secret. We can take it to our graves."

"I can't do this . . ." I was torn between my love for Christian and my desire for Brice. He continued to stroke my back in circular motions.

"I know in my heart that you can't say you don't still love me. I know you do, baby. I see it in your eyes."

I opened my mouth to speak, but nothing came out. I was speechless.

"Mia, don't say anything. Let me love you. Give me this one night. We've been given this opportunity for a reason, baby. Just me and you in our own little world." He kissed my neck and nibbled on my left earlobe—my hot spots.

Heat exploded between my legs.

Brice slowly turned my chair around and admired my breasts for a few seconds with pure lust in his sexy eyes. Then he got down on his knees and greeted them like long-lost friends. Each breast was given special attention. He placed each one tenderly in his mouth, one at a time, while my arms encircled his shoulders.

Within seconds, my nipples were swollen and sticking out, practically begging for his mouth and tongue to continue. Brice teased
one with his thumb, and the first moan escaped my lips. I was a lost
cause. Brice sucked, caressed and nibbled on my nipples and breasts
until I was so hot I could barely contain myself. I was out of control.
Totally out of control. He knew he had me when I voluntarily
opened my legs to reveal my womanhood to his searching hands.

Brice wasted no time in sliding up my short skirt, pushing my
black thong panties to the side and slipping in his finger. He noticed how hot and wet I was. My womanhood was blossoming like
a spring flower. Another moan escaped my lips when his two fingers explored further within my moist walls. Within seconds, my
skirt was untied and my panties were off. He frantically pulled me
to the edge of my seat and loved me with his fingers, tongue and
mouth while I called out his name over and over again, louder and
louder. I pulled his head down so he couldn't get away. It felt too
delicious.

Brice whispered, "I want to taste you again and again until you
come in my mouth." I threw my head back, wrapped my legs around
his neck and held on for the ride. And what a ride it was. Brice
didn't stop until I had come at least twice. As my eyes rolled back in
my head, I trembled uncontrollably in his arms.

"That's my girl; let it go. It feels good, doesn't it?"

Somehow, we ended up on the tiled floor and I was pulling, yanking, grabbing, frantically trying to get his shorts and shirt off. I desperately needed to feel him inside me, like my very existence
depended on Brice's being inside me. We were both breathing heavily by now and groping each other like there was no tomorrow. In
our minds, there wasn't. This was a onetime event.

When Brice finally entered me, I was so slippery wet that he
didn't stay in the first try. Then we started going at it like animals.
Believe me, we were not making love; we were fucking like two wild
beasts in heat. Brice was hitting it like there was no tomorrow, and I
was eagerly rising up to take each frantic thrust. Brice was hitting it
just right. Our moans were lust-filled and in line with the frantic

pace at which we were going. There was no gentleness; we were sat-
isfying a pure animalistic desire. We were fucking.

I vaguely remember chanting repeatedly. "Oh, yes, there, oh, yes,
oh, baby, right there, oh, yes. You the man!"

The entire time Brice was fucking me, I felt like I had to have
him inside me or I'd cease to exist. His hands were all over my body,
eager and strong, exploring, searching, and making up for lost years.
His tongue and mouth savored every touch. When we were finally
fulfilled, our massive orgasms came back-to-back with such force
and intensity that we collapsed on the floor intertwined, unable to
move for a few moments until our erratic breathing calmed down.
Amazing.

Brice broke the silence. "Damn, that was awesome. That was unbelievable." He stroked my face lovingly. He was still inside me. Then
he kissed me, hard, and I tasted myself. He smiled and I smiled back.

He pulled out, quietly got up, and I admired his gorgeous body in
all its splendor as he strolled to the bathroom. Brice brought back a
warm hand towel to wipe me off. He gently picked me up with no
effort and carried me to my guest bedroom, where we proceeded to
make love again . . . slowly and gently this time.

Right before Brice entered me, he said, "I've dreamed of this day
for so long. You just don't know. I never stopped loving you, Mia.
Never." When he looked into my eyes and lowered his mouth to kiss
me, I believed him as passion filled me to the brim.

O kay, I know you think I'm a one hundred percent, heartless D-O-G. If it walks like a dog and acts like a dog, then it must be . . . It's not like that at all. Not by a long shot. Damn, I didn't go over there with the intention of seducing Mia, my best friend's wife. My intention was to hang out with my partner for a minute, but as fate would have it, he wasn't home. After that, things just happened.

No, my dick didn't just fall into her sweetness. You know what I mean. I know I haven't been the perfect man. I've made a lot of mistakes in my lifetime. Haven't we all? I'm not proud of my actions and feel guilty as hell, but if I had it to do all over again, I would. Yeah, I would. With no hesitation.

For five years, I'd been waiting for that one moment in time. To hold Mia in my arms again. To express my undying love to her. It's true what they say—a few seconds can make your life. I love Mia, always have, and probably always will. That's my reality. Her being married to my best friend only complicates things.

What about Kree? I love her too. I do. I know I can't have it both ways. I can't have my cake and eat it too. I love Mia and Kree in entirely different ways. It's hard to explain, to put my feeling into words.

Mia is the woman for whom I'd lay down my life. She owns my heart to which I freely gave her the key years ago.

Kree . . . I love her dearly for her loyalty and her love for me. Kree was there when I needed someone. She has many of the wifely qualities that I'd love for Mia to have. Bottom line, Kree is a good and decent wife. I love her. I just don't love her with the same feverish passion as I do Mia. Who knows? If Mia had those same qualities, maybe we'd still be together. Life is funny like that.

Every relationship is like a piece of a puzzle that may or may not fit. Some fit better than others, but they don't complete the puzzle. Then you find another piece that fits, but not in the way the previous one did. So we are constantly searching for the pieces that complete the puzzle. When you find it, you hold on to it.

For the last five days since Mia and I made love, I haven't been able to eat, sleep or think straight. It's like I've been going around and around in circles. It takes me twice as long to do routine chores. I now realize how in tune Kree is with my emotions. She knows something is up, something is different, but she just doesn't know what. I've stayed away from Mia these last five days because I lied to her—one night wasn't enough. That one night only made me want her more. That was a teaser. Mia hasn't attempted to contact me either. I have no idea what's going through her head. That alone is killing me slowly.

I've been brushing off Christian left and right. He has called me a couple of times at work to invite me out to lunch, but I always lie to him and say that I'm too busy and can't get away. I can't face him. I know if I see him, guilt will be written all over my face. Believe it or not, I still love him like a brother. I never meant for this to happen. I know I've betrayed his trust. Life is funny like that; it has a crazy way of spiraling out of control. Anyway, something is going to have to give. And soon.

So, on the sixth night, I drove to Mia's place. I knew Christian was working late because I had spoken with him earlier. It was around eight P.M., the time Lyric was usually in bed and fast asleep. I'd convinced Kree that I was going out for a few drinks after I stopped by the office to look over some contracts. I had a few hours during which my whereabouts wouldn't be questioned if I played my cards right. I figured it was best not to call Mia first, because I didn't know what her reaction would be if I was headed over.

I parked a block away from their house and walked up the driveway. I didn't want any nosy neighbors checking out my car. After I rang the doorbell, Mia opened the door on the second ring and immediately pulled me inside the foyer.

"Brice, what are you doing here?" she asked frantically with her arms folded in front of her.

"Calm down, baby! No one saw me, and Christian is going to be at work for a while. Don't get all stressed out. Is Lyric sleeping?"

Mia nodded as I led her by the elbow into the living room. Based on the green throw lying on the sofa and Mia's disheveled appearance, I assumed she had been napping.

"Listen, Mia, we need to talk. Talk about the other night." We sat down together.

"Brice, there's nothing to talk about. It happened and I hope to God that neither Christian nor Kree ever finds out. What were we thinking? This could hurt a lot of people."

I looked into her big, beautiful brown eyes and lightly caressed her cheek. She didn't stop me. That was a good sign.

"I agree, baby. But the other night meant a lot to me. It was beautiful and special and made me realize how much I still care for you."

Mia looked down at her hands in her lap.

"Mia, say something. Talk to me." I gently lifted her chin back up.

"I don't know what to say. I . . . I mean, I thought about you a lot over the years. And we never really had closure," Mia said nervously as she stared at the far wall and not at me.

"Go on. Keep talking, baby. Get it all out. Let me know what you're thinking."

"I love Christian. With all my heart. But the other night, I guess I realized that a part of me had never stopped loving you either. After everything that happened . . ." She looked deep into my eyes. "Brice, what we did was wrong. It never should have happened."

"All I know is that holding you again made me feel complete. I felt a wholeness I haven't felt in years."

Cautiously, we reached for each other, seeking each other's lips. The kiss started out slowly, then gradually escalated into deep, hot, tongue-searing passion. Fire. Kisses like fire. I held Mia's face between my hands and kissed her like she held the key to my very existence. I wanted Mia to feel my love for her as I probed my tongue deeper and deeper into her warm, accepting mouth.

"Come here," I whispered as I pulled her even nearer.

Mia parted her lips again. By now, Mia was softly moaning, and I started a trail of wet kisses down her neck and pulled her T-shirt aside to expose more soft brown skin.

Mia reached under my T-shirt and timidly rubbed my back, up and down, just barely touching me with her fingernails. I had managed to pull her shirt over her head. She didn't have on a bra. As I sucked and licked her breasts, Mia leaned back against the sofa with her eyes closed. I pulled off her jeans and panties in one attempt. Her beauty never ceased to amaze me. I admired her body while I slowly undressed myself.

"Mia, look at me. Open your eyes. I need to know this is what you want."

Mia reluctantly opened her eyes, but she didn't answer my question or look at me. Her eyes were everywhere but on me.

"Mia, look at me. Look at my body." She raised her eyes to check me out.

"Now, I need to know, baby."

Mia attempted to pull me into her embrace as she placed my hand between her open legs. She was moist. I pulled away even though my dick was standing at full alert.

"Mia, we aren't going to do anything until I hear you say that you want me to make love to you."

"Don't make me beg, Brice," she said playfully with her eyes at half-mast. "You know."

"No, I don't. That's why I'm asking. I'm not kidding, Mia. I need to know that you want this, too. As much as I do," I said in a serious tone. "Tell me."

Mia hesitated for a few seconds, looking back down at her hands as if the answer were there. Then she looked back at me with confidence.

"Brice, I need to feel you inside me. Please make love to me so that I can sleep soundly tonight and know that I didn't imagine the other night. I need to know that this was all worth it."

With that, we retreated back into our little world where no one got hurt, to where there were no worries or regrets, to where we loved each other endlessly. However, as we would soon learn, that world existed only in our imaginations.

Brice is like a drug, and I'm addicted! A straight-up drug addict. I've had withdrawal symptoms for five years. I know what we've done—three times now—is totally wrong. I can't seem to stop myself; when Brice looks at me or touches me, I lose all control. My brain turns to mush. My body and heart betray me. I crave him, feen for him! I love Christian with everything I have and I know he doesn't deserve this. Yet I can't stop. I'm caught up.

I knew this reunion with Brice was a serious mistake. In the back of my mind, I knew I still loved him. Does that make me sick? I mean, the man used to beat the shit out of me. Yet he could make the best love to me, could have me begging for more, and still can. But even with the beatings, I knew he still loved me. I don't know; Brice and I were like oil and water. He loved me so much, but that love brought out the worst in him. His love came out in ugly ways: jealousy, possessiveness and control.

Five years later, Brice still has this control over my mind and body. When I'm with him, I can't think straight; he suffocates me, makes me high and makes me do crazy shit. Christian has been off the past few evenings. In fact, he has made sure he has the evenings off—just to please me. Yet I'm so confused that all I do is sleep. When I'm troubled, I sleep my life away. And Christian knows that. He knows something is very wrong. He just doesn't know what. Thank God.

I feel so guilty, so unworthy of Christian's love. Always have. Yet, when I think of Brice, my body trembles when it remembers— remembers his touch, his smell, his voice. I haven't made love to Christian since I've been with Brice. I'm afraid that I'll call out

Brice's name in the heat of passion or that my body won't respond. There's no way in hell that I can let Christian find out about this. It would kill him, and he would hate me. I couldn't live with him hating me. That would kill me.

If I'm really honest with myself, I'll admit that I've always felt unworthy of Christian's love, that he is too good for me. I came to him as damaged goods. Brice had done such a number on me that it was a wonder that I could love again. But I did. I love Christian so much. That's why I can't understand what's happening. So I sleep and keep everything inside.

I can't tell Sharon about this. What would she think of me? I've told her too many times how much I hate and despise Brice. No, Sharon wouldn't understand my spreading my legs for him. Mama is out of the question. I mean, you can't tell your mama that you're screwing the man who almost ruined your life. So now I sleep to hide from my emotions, from Christian and from myself.

Mama always says, "what's done in darkness comes to light." She has tons of these sayings that she quotes all the time. I've heard that one millions of times. Well, it didn't take long for the light to shine brightly. Christian found out the awful truth about me and Brice.

It was three and a half weeks after the affair had started. Christian came home from work earlier than usual one evening. Lyric was staying the night at Mama's house. She had been spending a lot of time over there lately. I was sleeping as usual; I hadn't even bothered to change out of my PJs.

Christian found me in the bedroom, lights off, in bed with the covers pulled up over my head.

"Mia, get up! We need to talk," he said in a demanding tone, yanking the covers back and shaking me by the shoulders.

Even in my sleepiness, I immediately knew that something was up. Christian didn't talk to me like that.

"Okay, okay. What's up?" I asked, wiping the sleep from my eyes and leaning back on my elbows.

"You tell me, Mia. What's up? Why all the sleeping? You don't want me to touch you. Why aren't you dressed? What's the deal?" There was urgency in his voice.

"I don't know what you're talking about. I haven't been feeling well lately. That's all." I looked down.

"Like hell! Don't lie to me, Mia," he screamed in my face.

Now I was wide-awake. I didn't say anything. I just cringed back against the sturdy bedpost.

"I've talked to our neighbors, the Petersons. I know Brice was over here three weeks ago. They described him perfectly. I also received an interesting phone call from Kree," he yelled, pacing back and forth from the bed to the mahogany dresser.

"What are you trying to say?" I asked in a tiny whisper.

"I'm not trying to say anything. I'm stating facts. You tell me, Mia! I'm going to ask you this just one time, and I want the damn truth!"

I quickly closed my eyes and said a prayer. I knew my life was going to end with his next question.

"Do you hear me, Mia? I want the truth. Are you capable of the truth?" he barked, taking me out of my reverie.

"Yes, I heard you." My eyes began to water, and big tears slid down my face and bounced off my cheeks.

"Did you sleep with Brice?" His voice cracked with emotion.

I couldn't look at him or answer the question. I dropped my head and wiped away tears from my eyes.

"Silence is golden. I guess that answers my question. Huh?" There was so much hurt and anger in his tone.

"I can't believe you'd do that to me, to us." He held his head in his hands and sat down on the edge of our bed.

I started sobbing uncontrollably.

"Don't cry now, Mia! Were you crying when Brice was fucking you? I want to hear you say it. Tell me that you let him fuck you. Say it!" He lunged in my direction.

I jumped back on my knees and pushed myself against the bedpost. For the first time ever, I was afraid of Christian.

"Say it!"

"Yes, I slept with Brice. Is that what you wanna hear? I'm so sorry, baby. I didn't . . ." I sobbed.

"Yeah, you are sorry. A sorry bitch!"

"Christian, please don't hate me. I made a mistake . . ."

"You know what? You are so pathetic, Mia. You make me sick to my stomach. You literally make me want to puke. You let Brice screw you after all that shit he put you through!" he screamed.

Again, I jumped back in fear. Christian was breathing fire and spewing venom.

"Dammit, Mia. As much as I want to, I'm not going to hit you. That's your problem. All these years, you've waited for the moment when I'd hit you. You've never totally trusted me or given me all your love. You held back a part of yourself, and I didn't care. I settled for what you could give me, for what you were capable of giving."

Silence. Heavy sobs.

"I'm not Brice. All men aren't like him. My love doesn't come with pain. Understand I'd never put my hands on you. I love— correction, loved—you too much for that," he said, near tears as he moved toward our dresser again.

"What are you doing?" I screamed, realizing he was taking out clothes.

"What do you think? What does it look like? I'm getting the hell out of here. I can't stand to see your fucking face." He pulled out an overnight bag from under the bed and started packing underwear, socks and a few shirts and pants.

I tried to put Christian's clothes back, but he pushed me away. My sobbing continued, and snot ran from my nose.

"Christian, don't leave me, baby. I love you! Please don't leave me. Please don't leave me!" I screamed, throwing myself at him. I was totally out of control. I was pathetic.

Christian pushed me off him. "You have a funny way of showing love. I don't need your kind of love, Mia!"

"You wanted this reunion, not me! You forced us together. You did this. I didn't want this. You wanted this, not me." I cried, jabbing him repeatedly in the chest.

Christian pushed me aside like I was nothing. "Yeah, Mia, I did. However, I didn't know you'd end up sleeping with Brice. Stupid me! I thought you'd remain faithful to me, not drop your drawers the first chance you got."

"It wasn't like that. Baby, stay here and let's work this out. I promise, it's over. It won't happen again. We can go to counseling . . . I'll do anything you say. I love you so much," I cried frantically as I clawed at his shirt.

"I don't give a fuck what you do! Don't you understand you betrayed me? You betrayed our marriage, our love." He pushed me, hard, back on the bed, picked up his black overnight bag and headed toward our bedroom door.

"Christian, don't leave me! I can't live without you." I sobbed into the sheet on the bed.

"Mia, grow up. Call your lover, sleep your life away. Better yet, go to hell! I don't care! I can't believe I thought you were special. I can't believe I once loved you," he said without even glancing back in my direction.

"Where are you going? Where will you stay?"

"Anywhere but here!"

The front door closed with a violent bang. With great effort, I inched myself backward on the bed and got back under the covers. I felt like nothing; Christian's words had reduced me to a feeling of worthlessness. I was suddenly cold, and felt so alone. I'm not sure how long I cried heart-wrenching sobs before I fell asleep.

Much later, I vaguely remembered the ringing of the phone pulling me out of my restless, fretful sleep. I didn't have the strength to answer. I heard the answering machine pick up and Mama's voice saying that she'd talked with Christian. She wanted me to call her as soon as possible, and said Lyric could stay with her for the night. The mention of Lyric's name brought a tiny smile to my dry, parched lips. Lyric, the one good thing left in my life. She'd be better over at Mama's house. I turned over and cried myself back to sleep. Images of an angry Christian played over and over in my mind throughout the night. Even in sleep, I felt the depth of his hate.

The next day, I managed to get out of bed around noon and took a long, hot shower. I looked a mess. My eyes were puffy and swollen from all the crying, and my hair was matted down and stinky. I attempted to eat a slice of toast with butter and drink some hot tea. Physically, I felt a little better; mentally, I was a wreck. Emotionally, I was devastated. I called Christian's job and was told he didn't come in. I placed several more calls, but no one had heard from or seen him. I was pulling my hair out with worry and concern.

I made the dreaded phone call to Mama and explained in between fresh sobs what had happened. To my surprise, she wasn't judgmental or shocked. Mama didn't say "I told you so" or anything like that. She did say that she was here for me and always would be. Mama also agreed to keep Lyric for another day until I got myself together. Lyric didn't need to see me in the emotional state I was in. Children pick up on more than we think.

"Pray, Mia. Prayer changes things," Mama stated.

"Okay, Mama, I will."

"And I'm praying for you too, sweet pea."

"Thank you, Mama."

"We fall down, but we can get back up."

"I know, Mama. Thank you."

With that, I solemnly hung up the phone.

For the remainder of the day, I moped around the house, not doing much of anything. I kept expecting to hear from Christian, hoping he'd tell me that we could work this out or that he'd forgiven me. His phone call never came, and I sank deeper and deeper into a depressed state. Late evening found me crashed on the sofa, covered up with my favorite green throw, in front of the TV, which I wasn't watching, with an uneaten sandwich and soda. I couldn't keep anything in my stomach.

When I heard the doorbell ring, I got a burst of energy. I jumped off the sofa, expecting to see Christian, who'd forgiven me for my transgressions. I swung open the door. Brice was standing there. We just stared at each other like two strangers.

"May I come in?"

I didn't say anything. I walked away, defeated, sat back on the sofa and drew my knees up to my chest.

"Mia, I'm sorry. I'm so very sorry. I didn't mean for any of this to happen," he said in all sincerity as he sat down next to me.

"Your wife called Christian. How did she find out? I thought you said you were being careful."

"I thought I was. She followed me one night. Can you believe that? Kree thought I was acting strange, and she followed me over here."

"Oh," was all I could say.

"I thought I was being careful, baby. I honestly didn't mean for this to blow up in our faces like it has."

"I have nothing now. It doesn't even matter anymore. It happened. It *has* blown up in our faces, and Christian hates me. You should have seen how he looked at me. Like I was nothing. He's never . . ." Fresh tears streamed down my face.

Brice pulled me to him and consoled me as if I were a small child. We sat like that for a while, with Brice holding me. No words were spoken. None were necessary. The only sounds were my cries and Brice's gentle assurances.

When I finally looked up at him, I saw pure anguish etched on his handsome face. I knew then that he was truly hurting as well. I lightly touched his face and traced his five-o'clock shadow with my fingers. We kissed almost timidly. When Brice stood and held out his hand, I took it and followed him into the guest bedroom. He undressed me and then himself. We made love *slowly* for hours. There was no need to rush. I felt the love in Brice's every touch. Afterward, I fell into a deep sleep, wrapped in his arms. For a few hours, I felt safe.

Much like the night before, the ringing of the phone pulled me back to reality. Brice didn't want me to answer it, but I thought it might be Christian. I yanked it up on the third ring.

"Hello."

There was a pause.

"Put my husband on the phone!"

I handed the phone to Brice, pulled up the sheet to cover my nakedness and turned my back to him.

"It's your wife."

I don't know what Brice said to her. I remember he was angry and loud. Very loud. I tuned it all out and realized that Christian still hadn't bothered to call me. When Brice was finished, he gave the phone back to me, apologizing. Calmly, I placed it back on the cradle. Everything was surreal.

"Baby, I'm sorry about that." He pulled me back to him and kissed my forehead.

"No, I'm sorry. Go home, Brice. Go home to your wife."

Brice started to protest. I held up my upturned hand.

"Please, Brice. Just go home."

He knew it was pointless to argue with me. Brice kissed me on the cheek and left. I didn't bother to see him out. I heard the door close softly. I was thankful that sleep rescued me from my living nightmare and wrapped its safe, comforting warmth around me.

Another couple of weeks had gone by and the start of the new school year was fast approaching. I was living the life of a recluse. I didn't go anywhere. I didn't do anything. My life, if that's what it was, was spent mostly in bed. I didn't have the strength or the will to do anything more. I wasn't eating; I couldn't keep anything down. I was always nauseous or throwing up. Mama had come over and cleaned up the place. She said I ought to be ashamed of living in a pigsty. Mama was still taking care of Lyric for me, because I just didn't have the patience or the frame of mind to do it myself.

Sharon had stopped by a few times as well. Shortly after Christian left me, Sharon stopped by unexpectedly to find me sitting in the dark. She washed my hair, which was starting to grow back, and gave me a pedicure and manicure. She painted my nails and toes bright red, my favorite color, which did nothing to help my mood. Most of the talking was done by her; I had nothing to say.

"Mia?"

"Huh?"

"I know you're hurting."

I didn't say anything.

"You know I'm here for you, girlfriend. I love you like a sister. This whole situation is tearing me up too."

"I know."

"Don't beat yourself up too much; you're human. You bleed red like the rest of us. You had a moment of weakness."

No response from me.

"Do you still love Christian?"

"Yes."

"Is it over with you and Brice?"

"Yes."

"Okay, we'll get through this together, girlfriend."

At first Brice called me constantly, but I told him I didn't want to see him anymore. We'd hurt too many people. It was over before it started. I told him to work things out with Kree, because that's what I wanted to do with Christian. For now, he accepted that. He had enough problems of his own at home to deal with.

Christian . . . Sometimes, I'd sleep with one of his shirts to smell him next to me. It comforted me. I hadn't heard from him or seen him since the night he left me. He was always unavailable at his job. I got the message loud and clear. The one time that Sharon had managed to get me out of the house, Christian came by to retrieve some more of his clothes.

I heard, through the grapevine, that Christian was sharing an apartment with one of his employees, Michael. Mama saw him whenever he dropped by to take Lyric out. She said he didn't look good at all; he had lost a lot of weight and had a permanent frown.

Another month had passed and I knew it wouldn't be long before Brice dishonored my wishes to leave me alone. I had taken a leave of absence from my teaching job and was sitting around in shorts and a T-shirt. I heard the doorbell ring. I had actually gotten dressed that day. I saw Brice through the peephole. He looked like nothing would make him go away. I didn't want the drama or have the strength to argue, so I opened the door and let him in.

"Brice, what do you want? Please leave me alone." I walked over to the kitchen table.

"Mia, just hear me out. I promise if you'll just talk to me, I won't bother you anymore if you don't want me to."

I stared at him. I guess he took that as his cue to continue.

"I love you, Mia, and that is never going to change. I'm suffering like you are. Kree threw me out of the house, and—"

"What? I'm sorry, Brice. We were so reckless. We didn't think about the consequences of our actions. That's our problem; we just never thought about anything else."

"We could still be together. You and me. It's not too late. We could make it work this time."

"No, no, we can't. My life is in a total shambles. This isn't going to work. We can't go back and reclaim the past. The past is just that—the past. I finally realize that."

"We could make it work, baby, if we tried. We could go away and start over. Make a new life for ourselves . . ."

"No, Brice. It wouldn't work. We could never be happy knowing we'd hurt people in the process."

For once, Brice was quiet and reflective.

"Let's put everything on the table. I might as well tell you. I may be pregnant . . . with your baby," I shouted before I lost my nerve.

"What? Oh, my God. Baby, are you sure?" Brice was excited as he searched my face for the truth.

"I'm not a hundred percent sure, but if I am, I'm not having it. I can't."

"What? What are you saying? Mia, don't kill my baby. Please don't kill my flesh and blood. Tell me you aren't saying that."

"Brice, I'm sorry, but I've already made up my mind. I've thought long and hard on this. Long and hard. It hasn't been an easy decision, but it's the only way. Anyway, I don't know for sure if I am pregnant."

"Mia, I'm begging you. Don't kill my baby, our baby," he cried as he gently touched my stomach.

I started to cry. "Brice, I can't handle this right now. I'm so close to losing it. So close. I can't handle more drama. Please go. Please."

"Okay. I'm going to go, because I don't want to bring any more pain your way. I've already dealt you enough. I've been doing a lot of thinking these past few weeks myself. Bottom line, everything I've ever said to you was real. I always have and always will love you, Mia. I'll go to my grave loving you." He held my hands in his.

"I love you too, Brice, but sometimes love just isn't enough."

Brice looked at me with sadness and nodded. He stood up and I walked him to the front door. He realized there wasn't much more that he could say. At the door, he hesitated for a moment. He stared at me as if commiting my face to memory. Brice pulled me into a strong embrace, which lasted for a few seconds, and rubbed my back. He kissed me on the cheek and looked at me one last time.

"My love for you was always real, baby. I can't force you to have my baby, but know that I want it more than life itself. I can't believe a part of me is growing inside you. It's a testament to our great love." He caressed my cheek and smiled, but his smile never reached his eyes.

With that, Brice turned and walked out the door and my life for the last time. For some reason, I watched him until he drove away and was out of sight.

Later that night, I was in my usual spot on the sofa, feeling sorry for myself, when the doorbell rang. I thought it might be Brice coming back to make me change my mind about the baby. I was surprised to see Kree standing in my doorway. Her appearance shocked me. Kree had a black eye, a bruised face and swollen lips. She was disheveled and crying silently as she pushed her hair out of her face. Without thinking, I hurriedly opened the front door, full of concern.

"Oh, God! Kree, come in. What happened? Did Brice do this to you?"

"You, that's what happened! Save your sympathy."

I stood back, suddenly fearful of the venom behind her words.

"My marriage—my life—was going well before you came back into the picture. You couldn't leave well enough alone. You had to have my man too."

"Kree, I'm so sorry. It just happened. You have to try to understand; Brice and I had a unique history. We never really had closure after our divorce. And it just happened."

"It just happened and you're sorry," Kree said nonchalantly.

I nodded my head, because words wouldn't come out.

"That's all you have to say? Unbelievable! I came over here for answers. To see what you had to give him that I didn't or couldn't. And all you can say is that you're sorry."

She shook her head in disbelief and pity. "Mia, you are a self-centered, self-righteous, self-absorbed, conniving *bitch!*" Kree slapped the hell out of me. As I screamed out, I fell back a step from the force of her hand. I held my left cheek as she fled from my front door. I closed the door, still holding my stinging cheek, and retreated back to the sofa and my favorite comforter. I was too cried out to even cry. Once again, sleep was my salvation.

Christian

I believe that you shouldn't be so eager to find out a secret. It could change your life forever.

—Author Unknown

I believe that our background and circumstances may have influenced who we are, but we are responsible for who we become.   —Author Unknown

I avoided Mia like the plague. To me, she *was* the plague. Unselfishly, I served her my heart on a silver platter, and now my heart was an oozing, raw, open wound. I hadn't seen her since our confrontation. I couldn't. That girl busted my heart wide-open. I'm no punk. I'm a man and supposed to be strong and hard and not cry. But I'm not going to lie: This betrayal has hit me hard, because I didn't even see it coming. I was secure in our love, Mia's love for me, but I guess Brice had a tighter pull on her heartstrings.

I've gone through every emotion possible, from hating her, to cursing her, to blaming myself for bringing them back together, to crying in my sleep, to not being able to work or sleep or eat. Yes, Mia has taken me through some major changes, and I despise her for that. As much as I loved my moms and as much as her death affected me, this situation has hit me even harder. And every time I see Lyric, I see Mia in her. It's bittersweet because Lyric keeps me sane; she's my one joy.

One night, I parked outside our house for hours, like you see in the movies—you know, lights off, hunched down in my seat, just staring at our dark bedroom window to get a glimpse of Mia. Deep down inside, I also wanted to witness for myself her and Brice to-gether. However, he was a no-show that night. As much as I tried to hate Mia, a part of me still craves to be near her again, but I stay away because I can't trust her and, without trust, I can't be with her.

Brice. I want to kill him! No-good muthafucka! In fact, when I first found out about him and Mia, I actually parked in front of his office building early one morning to catch him on his way to work. I was going to put a serious hurting on his sorry ass that he wouldn't soon forget; I was literally seeing red. I sat in my car for quite a while, but, as fate would have it, Brice never came to work that day.

Eventually, my anger subsided, and I realized what a mistake I was about to make. Lyric needs me. I need to set an example for her if her own mother can't. And besides, I wasn't going to give Brice the satisfaction of going upside his head with a baseball bat and going to jail. He's not worth it.

It's been almost two months since I left Mia. I've kept myself busy, working all the time. During my time off, I work out and spend quality time with Lyric. I pick her up at my moms-in-law's and we'll do the father-daughter bonding thing. My mother-in-law is cool; she's not interfering or taking sides in the situation. She did inform me that Lyric spends more time with her than she does with Mia.

My pain has subsided a bit. I think it is a part of me now, like an arm or leg. The pain is familiar now. I relish it.

I was surprised to receive a phone call from Kree yesterday at work. We talked for a few minutes about trivial stuff as if our lives hadn't been turned upside down, inside out. She wanted to know if I could drop by later that evening. Kree wanted to talk and was even going to throw in a home-cooked meal. That sealed the invite. I didn't think her invitation was strange. I agreed and told her I'd be there around seven P.M. I needed to go back to Michael's apartment, a place I was calling home nowadays, to shower and change. I figure Kree needs an ear or two to vent in. After all, we're both in the same boat; we're the victims.

I arrived at her crib around seven twenty. I rang the doorbell, and

Kree greeted me at the door looking simply gorgeous. She wore tight-fitting denim pants and a sleeveless red shirt. I don't know how I expected her to look, down and out maybe—but she was just the opposite. We were all wrong about her. Kree was strong and a true survivor. I got the feeling that whatever happens, she'll survive this. No doubt.

Kree's long hair was loose in wavy, spiral curls that frame her lovely face. She welcomed me with a big smile and a hug that lasted a little too long for comfort.

"Hi, Kree. How are you, baby girl?" I gave her a welcoming hug back.

"I'm taking it one day at a time. I have my good and bad days. Keeping busy. I'm teaching a dance class at Spelman College's after-school program.

"Good for you."

"What about you? How are you, Christian?" She stood back to really look at me.

"About the same, keeping busy."

She invited me in, and I took a seat on her new-smelling leather sofa.

"New furniture?" I asked.

"Yeah, I totally redecorated in here and in our . . . my bedroom. There were just too many reminders of him."

We were both quiet, lost in our own private thoughts.

Kree asked, "Have you seen him or her lately?"

"No, I have no desire to. They deserve each other. Good riddance."

"I agree. He's moved into an apartment near his office, and life is going on for him. As long as he sends me my checks, I don't care. I decided I deserve so much more for myself! He came over here one night, trying to sweet-talk me and get some. Not!

"I hear his business is taking off. That's good, because he'll be receiving divorce papers soon. I intend to get my fair share. Anyway, tonight we are not going to talk about them. Okay? As far as we are concerned, they don't even exist. All of this was just a real bad dream. Anyhow, I just wanted to see how you were doing. I always liked you, Christian; you seemed real."

"Thank you. I've always liked you too, Kree."

"Do we have a deal?"

"A deal?"

"Yeah, let's enjoy tonight and not mention them."

"You got it, baby girl." I gave her a genuine smile. It kinda felt funny, because I hadn't smiled in a while.

Kree and I enjoyed a delicious meal of baked trout, rice, and a garden salad and drank chardonnay. We laughed and talked and laughed even more, like good friends. It felt nice. Real good. I wasn't thinking about Mia or Brice.

"Christian, I hope you still have room for dessert. I went to the deli around the corner and bought some key lime pie."

"Sounds good. You're spoiling me. I haven't eaten like this in a long time. This was great! Thanks, Kree." I kissed her on the cheek.

"Give me a minute and I'll serve it in the living room."

I retreated to the living room, laid my head back on the sofa and closed my eyes. The radio was playing softly in the background—the Quiet Storm on V-103. I heard Kree moving around in the kitchen.

I must have drifted off for a few minutes. I opened my eyes when I heard Kree softly call out my name. She was standing there stark naked in all her glory. The lady was sexy as hell, with a banging body: big breasts, firm ass, tiny waist. I did a double take and instantly got an erection.

"Kree? Kree, what are you doing? As much as I'd love to, let's not take it there. I think you need to put on some clothes. I can only take so much temptation. Right now, you've got my nature rising. I'm sorry if I gave you the impression—"

"I thought . . . I . . . I'm sorry." She turned and ran down the hallway in tears.

I gave her a few minutes to pull herself together. Then I walked down the hallway to find her bedroom door closed. I could hear her crying. I knocked softly and called out her name.

"Kree? Kree, may I come in?"

"The door's unlocked," I heard her say.

When I walked in, Kree was sitting on the edge of her bed in a silk bathrobe.

"I feel so foolish. So stupid," she said, biting her nail.

"Kree, no. Don't feel that way. You're a beautiful, intelligent woman."

"I thought we could pay them back if we got together. Give them a dose of their own medicine."

"Then we'd be lowering ourselves to their level. What would that say about us?"

She just looked up at me with sad, pitiful eyes.

"Kree, believe me, if circumstances were different . . . Like I said, you're a beautiful, sexy woman. Any man would give his right arm to make love to you."

"Any man but you, right?" She twisted a strand of her hair around a finger.

"If I went there tonight, I'd just be using you, and I care about you too much to do that."

"You still love her, don't you? After everything they've done to us, you still love her."

I didn't answer. My silence said it all.

"You know Mia doesn't deserve you. You're a good man, Christian. She doesn't realize what a gem she had in you."

"I guess not or I wouldn't be here. Anyway, are you okay now?"

"Yeah, yeah, I am," she said as if she were contemplating something.

"Look, it's getting late. I should be going. I have a full day tomorrow, but I'm here if you need me. You know my number."

"I do, thanks. Wait, Christian, I need to talk to you. I want to tell you a story." She took a deep breath. "I know you still love Mia even if you don't want to admit it."

"I—"

"You don't even have to answer. Just listen carefully to my story. As you know, Mia is not my favorite person in the world. Even before I met her, I felt I was living in her shadow. In my heart, I knew Brice wasn't over her. And as much as I hate to admit it, I understand the pull Brice has on her. It took me a while to come to that realization, but I understand. And . . . I don't hate her as much."

I sprawled across Kree's bed and waited out of curiosity for her to continue. I had a feeling her story was going to shed some light on our present situation.

"I have never told anyone this story before—I was too ashamed—but after I finish, you'll understand why I can relate to why Mia did what she did." Kree took a deep breath and continued the story.

"After dating Brice for about a year in Germany, I knew I loved him with all my heart. I wanted to spend the rest of my life with him. Everything was perfect. Too perfect. We communicated, we had tons of fun together, we shared common goals and dreams. Our sex life was great, but Brice kept talking about taking it to the next level. He had this fantasy about having a threesome with me and another woman. Brice explained that he had had ménage à trois before, but it was just with casual acquaintances. With me—with us—this would take our lovemaking, our intimacy, to the next level, he said. I heard this over and over until he finally persuaded me to do it for him."

Kree scrutinized me closely, took a deep breath, and continued. "He chose this lady, Jade, that he knew from one of the bars he frequented. She was really lovely, sexy and the complete opposite of me. She wasn't reserved or inhibited, to say the least. Brice and I had discussed the rules before I agreed to do it. The number one rule was that she couldn't touch me. He could touch me, he could touch her, but she couldn't touch me under any circumstances. Brice agreed—only he would be making love to me."

Kree closed her eyes as the memories flooded her.

"The night of our date came. We'd checked into a luxury hotel for the night and had dinner and drinks. I had a buzz going when we arrived back to the room—room 203. I figured that I needed to be high to carry it out. I was nervous as hell. We got back to the room and Jade was there. She'd already set the mood. You know, dim light, candles, the whole nine yards. Everything started happening quickly.

"Brice took control as usual. By now, we had all undressed, checking out one another's bodies. There was nervous laughter. We were on the king-size bed and Brice started kissing me, real passionate kisses, and then he'd kiss Jade. Things were getting hot and heavy as he went back and forth between us. Jade and I would sit there and wait for our turn. Then Brice stopped, jumped off the bed, naked, and quickly pulled up a chair from the desk and placed it in front of the bed."

By now, Kree's voice was trembling. She struggled to continue.

"He was sitting there like he had center-stage seats at a performance or something. Brice coaxed me to kiss Jade. I said no, because he had promised me that I wouldn't have to touch her. He finally talked me into just kissing her. Jade's warm tongue was in my mouth, kissing me like Brice had just done. Brice watched with no emotion. After a while, he told me to touch Jade. This time, I refused. So he told Jade to touch me. I begged her not to, but I guess she had seen something in his eyes that convinced her to follow his instructions instead of mine.

"By now Brice had moved back to the bed. Anyway, Jade started to touch me with her hands, mouth and tongue. She started from my neck and worked her way slowly down. She left wet, moist spots as she went down. What did I do? I sat there and stared at Brice while he watched us and fondled her breasts. I didn't take my eyes off him. The scene was turning him on. As Jade continued, I started to cry uncontrollably. She hesitated, but Brice commanded her to continue.

"He told me to lie down and open my legs. I wouldn't do it. Brice said it again in that military, commanding voice of his. I leaned back and spread my legs, and Jade was down between my legs, with her tongue and fingers going in and out. I was crying while Brice watched and enjoyed it. Jade was making this moaning, slurping sound over and over.

"Brice caressed my breast with his hands and mouth. Jade was still busy, working my clit. Brice inserted a finger into my wetness. My body betrayed me and I came, came hard. He finally pushed Jade away from me and climbed on top of her. I tried to get up and walk away, but Brice pulled me back down by my wrist and gave me that look. I lay there crying beside the two of them while he screwed her. I heard all the groans and moans and I knew the exact moment he came in her. Afterward, he acted like nothing had happened.

"The next day, he sent me a dozen red roses, and I pushed that night into the dark recesses of my mind. Brice got his wish and was satisfied. So I was happy. That night was never mentioned again. Months later, when he asked me to marry him, I accepted. I didn't even hesitate for a second. I married him," she said with no emotion, and then burst out crying.

"Kree, don't cry. It's going to be okay. Don't cry. You didn't deserve that." I rubbed her back through her thin robe.

"I'm sorry. I guess I never allowed myself to think about that night. I blocked it all out, and Brice never took me back to that bar and I didn't see Jade ever again. I guess what I'm trying to say is that Brice has this hold on women and gets them to do whatever he wants. They—we—want to please him. So I can understand how Mia got caught up with him."

When I was sure Kree was really okay, I let myself out after thanking her for an enjoyable and enlightening evening. Kree left me with much to think about.

Another two weeks had passed since my dinner with Kree. I finally made my decision: I was going to see Mia. It was time. I couldn't hide from her forever. It was time for some closure in my life. Actually, Mia's moms had asked me to check on her. Apparently, Mia wasn't doing well; she was sinking deeper into a depression and finding it harder and harder to take care of Lyric.

I pulled up in front of the brick, ranch-style house which used to be my home. It hadn't been that long, but everything looked different. The lawn needed cutting and the hedges needed trimming. Mia's rosebush was dead. I had planted that for her when we first moved into the house. It was supposed to be symbolic of our love.

After a few minutes, I slowly walked up the driveway, not knowing what to expect behind the closed doors. I rang the doorbell and held my breath as I mentally prepared myself. *Okay, here we go.* Mia opened the door on the third ring. She stood there for a few seconds and just stared at me like she was seeing a ghost.

"Hi, Mia. May I come in?" I found my voice again.

She kinda nodded and turned to walk into the living room, expecting me to follow. Walking behind her gave me a moment to compose myself and check her out. Dressed in sweats and a gray T-shirt, Mia had changed. She was still beautiful, but she seemed more mature. She had lost a lot of weight. Mia had always been petite, but now she was just flat-out skinny. Her hair had grown out some and wasn't as short as before. It wasn't really in a style; it just hung from her head. It was funny, because Mia and Kree looked even more alike now.

Mia sat in the recliner across from the sofa, hands primly folded in her lap, and stared at me without uttering a word. She hadn't cracked a smile.

"How have you been? Did you get the money I sent?"

"I'm okay. I'm taking a leave of absence from Fairfield until . . . Yes, thanks for the money," she said in a monotone voice.

"Yeah, no problem. I couldn't have my daughter living on the streets."

"No, you couldn't have that."

"Where is she?"

"Sleeping."

Mia answered my questions with as few words as possible, looking down at her hands. She was afraid to look into my eyes. Something in my heart lurched forward.

"Listen, Mia. I'm not going to lie; your moms is worried about you. Why aren't you eating? You've lost a lot of weight."

"I wish Mama would leave me alone about eating. I don't have an appetite. I can't keep anything down most of the time," she said, shrugging her bony shoulders.

"Well, you haven't had one of my famous omelets, bacon and toast in a while." I smiled at her.

She didn't smile back. "I guess not."

"And your moms is concerned about you."

Mia just shrugged her bony shoulders.

"Listen, go and do what you were doing; don't mind me. I'm going to take a quick peek at my baby doll and then I'm going to whip you up one of those omelets."

"Christian, you don't have to . . ."

"I know, Mia. I want to."

"Thank you."

"You're welcome."

As she started to walk up the hallway, I called out her name. She turned.

"Your hair. Are you letting it grow out for him?"

"No, I'm not. It was over between me and him before it even started. I haven't seen Brice in weeks; I told him to leave me alone, and, surprisingly, he has."

"Yeah, now that everything and everyone is fucked up." I felt my temper rising.

Mia quickly left. I guess she didn't want to see me lose my temper again. I heard her moving around in the bathroom as she took her shower and changed into her pajamas. She shyly entered the kitchen just as I was finishing up. She resembled a little girl, with her hair pulled back in a ponytail. Mia started to clean up the kitchen, which was in disarray. In fact, I had a chance to look around, and the entire house was not too tidy. That wasn't like Mia.

"No, you sit down. I'll take care of the mess. Eat." I placed a full plate of hot food in front of her, along with a big glass of cold milk. For the first time, I saw a hint of a smile.

When she finished eating, I had washed the dishes in the sink.

"Thanks, Christian. I'm not someone for whom you'd want to

do any great acts of kindness. I know you are doing this for Mama. Thanks for the gesture."

"No, actually I'm doing this for me. Because I want to. Come sit down, Mia; we need to talk. Really talk for once."

I held out my hand and she took it with hesitation. I felt chills when our hands touched. Mia was so fragile; Brice had done a serious number on her. She was an emotional basket case. I almost felt sorry for her. Almost.

I led her over to the sofa. We sat side by side this time, and cried and talked and cried some more into the early-morning hours. A lot of words were spoken that should have been said months earlier. For once, Mia expressed her true feelings to me. Was it too late? I couldn't say. I left knowing one thing: I still loved Mia.

Mia

I believe that sometimes the people you expect to kick you when you're down, will be the ones to help you get back up.
                                                    —Author Unknown

Christian literally saved me. His visit gave me back my life. I had given up. Lyric was the only reason I woke up each morning, but I wasn't really living. Christian gave me the will to live again because he no longer hated me. I went back to Fairfield and did the one thing I loved to do—teach. By the way, I wasn't pregnant. Thank God. My ob-gyn told me that many times when women are under a great deal of stress, our cycles temporarily stop.

I also contacted a psychologist to help me deal with some of my issues. Losing my dad at a young age and growing up with an alcoholic mom contributed to my lack of self-esteem. I had my first session the other day. I probably went through a box of Kleenex. I couldn't stop crying.

Mama and Sharon have been my angels in disguise. They have been very supportive.

Mama babies both me and Lyric, and Sharon keeps me laughing over her usual antics. I'm trying to get my life back on track so I can be a mother to whom Lyric can look up to. I want her to grow into a strong, independent woman. So I have to become one.

Brice has tried to contact me a couple of times, but I won't return his calls. There's really nothing more to say. It's over. The final chapter has been written for us. Well, I did leave a message on his answering machine at work to tell him I wasn't pregnant. I know— I took the coward's way out.

I admit that I still think about him. A lot. My psychologist, Dr. Barnett, and I are going to discuss why I still care about Brice after what happened in our past together. I remember the details of the last time I saw him, when we said our final good-bye. For some reason, it sticks out in my mind.

Christian may not love me anymore, but at least he doesn't hate me. That means the world to me. I see him at least once a week when he drops by to pick up Lyric. He doesn't stay long. So far, Christian hasn't served me divorce papers, but he hasn't moved back in either. I try to keep hope alive. That's all I have for now.

My life is slowly moving back toward the light. But, sometimes, we have to take three steps backward in order to take two steps forward. We have to crawl before we can walk. I would soon learn the true meaning behind those words.

Christian gave me the news! I'll never forget that day as long as I live. Once again, my life went spiraling out of control. It started out as a routine, normal Friday evening. The six-o'clock news was ending. I was drying a load of clothes. Dinner dishes were in the dishwasher. Lyric was over at Mama's house. I was enjoying some "me" time at home. The doorbell rang and I was surprised to see Christian on my doorstep. Based on his expression, I knew something was drastically wrong when I opened the door. He pulled me into a crushing embrace.

"What's wrong, Christian? Tell me. What happened?"

He didn't say anything, only hung his head.

"Christian? You're scaring me. Are Lyric and Mama all right?"

"There was a car accident, and Brice . . . Brice is dead," he said in a trembling voice as he lowered his head again.

"What?" I screamed, frantically searching his face for the truth. "What are you saying?"

"I'm sorry, Mia. He's gone. They say it was instant."

"No, no, I don't believe you! I don't believe you! You're lying!" I screamed over and over, pounding my fists against his chest. Christian managed to restrain me by my thin wrists. The next thing I felt was a lovely, calming blackness engulfing me as I fell to the floor and collapsed. A welcoming blackness. I felt no more pain.

Much of the funeral was a blur as I sat next to Sharon, picking up pieces of the preacher's eulogy. I didn't see faces, only images of color: flashes of black, shades of gray, specks of blue. I was pretty drugged up, compliments of Dr. Barnett. Surprisingly, I didn't even cry; I was all cried out. I didn't have a single tear left. A numbness had descended upon me. Oddly enough, I felt at peace.

The grave site was even more of a blur. Everything was surreal. The preacher was saying something about everything happening for a reason. "It was in God's plan"? I didn't want to hear that. Yet I desperately needed an explanation or a reason why this tragedy had happened. My mind wandered to Brice, the alive, vibrant Brice. Even in death, Brice got the last word.

I discovered that Christian, Kree and myself had received e-mails from him. He had e-mailed us before his tragic accident. I will always cherish mine; it started my cleansing process. Brice freed me. It was his final gift to me. It read:

Mia,

I'm truly sorry for all the pain I've caused in your life. I hope that you'll remember the good times, too. There were many. Believe it or not, I loved you with everything I had. I know I had a hard way of showing it, but I did. Sometimes, unfortunately, we learn at our fathers' feet.

I think I loved you the first day I saw you; you were so beautiful and still are. Every man, if he's lucky, finds a woman who owns his heart, who gives him meaning in life. You were mine, Mia. With no hesitation, I willingly gave you my heart. You were my piece of the puzzle that fit. Know that.

I will always love you, Mia. I'll go to my grave loving you.

Now, that's love. Your face will be the last one I see in my mind, and I'll know I'm in heaven. Yeah, even in death, I'll be loving you.

A lot of times when you love someone, you have to set them free, so I'm setting you free. Find happiness, Mia. Find Christian. I wish you nothing but love, true happiness and, most of all, peace.

Forever yours,

Brice

Christian,

This is truly hard for me. I was never any good at expressing my feelings like this. At this point, I know that you really couldn't give a damn. Man, I've made so many mistakes in my lifetime, so many. Too many to even count on two hands.

I'm asking your forgiveness. Believe it or not, I didn't plan for this to happen. It just did. I know that is lame, but it's true. Please don't blame Mia; I shoulder all the responsibility. I honestly didn't move back home to wreck two households and a lifelong friendship. That wasn't in my plans—my grand scheme of things.

I've always loved you like a brother. I think you are the only male I've ever loved besides my father, and most of the time, as you know, that was a love-hate relationship. They didn't call us the "Two Musketeers" in school for nothing. I know I stepped way over the line, and, now there's no going back for us. I'll regret that until the day I die.

I understand if you can't find it in your heart to forgive me. Really I do. But please forgive Mia. She loves you so much, and if it's any consolation, she didn't want to hurt you. Neither did I. Things just quickly got out of hand; we had too many ties that bind. Love can touch us one time and last for a lifetime.

You're a good man, partner. Decent. I know your moms is looking down, proud of the man you've become. You've brought much joy to my life. Find your way back to Mia and have a happy, prosperous life. Peace.

One love,

Brice

That was the e-mail Brice had sent me. My last connection with him. I didn't know whether to laugh or cry. I still couldn't believe my man was gone. After all that had gone down, I never wished him dead. If I'm honest with myself, I never stopped loving him through it all.

It was hard, real hard, seeing him in that cold steel casket. Flowers were everywhere. The somber organ and piano music was playing. The realization that I would never have the opportunity to speak with him again, in anger or in joy, hurt me to the core. It still hasn't fully sunk in. Life isn't fair. That's the one true lesson I've learned.

I have all this pent up anger and these emotions and I can never tell him my feelings to his face.

The police report listed his death as an accident. Just a tragic, senseless accident. I don't know. I don't think Brice was distraught enough to take his own life. He was much stronger than that. But I've gone by the accident site myself several times, and there aren't any skid marks. Supposedly, Brice lost control of his vehicle, hit the guardrail, and went over the embankment. Instant death. End of story.

Unfortunately, it's not the end of the story. Vivica took it hard; her agonizing cries chilled me to the bone at his funeral. So much pain. They say it's hard for a mother to bury her child. The mother feels that she should go first. Brice's pops didn't really know what was going on, since his illness has taken a turn for the worse. I feel Brice and his father were at peace with each other.

Mia. I don't know where her head or heart is right now. Only time will tell. She has a supportive network of females. So she'll be okay.

To everyone's surprise, Kree has been getting on with her life. I know she loved Brice, but she's holding up. She's a strong lady, a pillar of strength. After meeting her moms, I see where she gets it. It just took longer for it to kick in. I guess it takes certain situations for us to realize how resilient we are. Life is funny like that.

The love of my life is gone forever. Forever. I still can't believe it. Even though we were separated, I knew he was across town. I could still pick up the phone and call him or drop by his office. I never did any of those things after our separation, but I knew I could if I wanted to. The last time we talked, we were civil. However, we both knew our marriage was over.

The funeral was nice, as far as funerals go. As I sat in the front pew, dressed in black, with Moms by my side, I realized Brice had a lot of people who cared about and respected him. People had flown in from all over the country, and one man had come from overseas. There wasn't an empty seat.

I glanced at the many faces that crossed my path that day, realizing that no one could feel the loss worse than myself, Christian or Miss Mia. Christian was giving the appearance of being strong, but I knew different. Regardless of what had happened, Brice was like a brother to him and vice versa. Mia was hanging on by the skin of her teeth. She had lost so much weight; she looked like a lost child. I couldn't even hate her anymore. She loved him as much as I did. It's not often that a man finds two women who would give up everything for him. We both paid the price.

As for me, I'm discovering myself. I'm stronger than I thought; I'm a survivor. When Brice had the affair, I thought my life was over. Then I realized I had other options. My life could be over or I could get up, hold my head high, and go on living. I could win or lose. I chose to win. And live.

It's been four weeks since the homegoing service. I reread the letter he had e-mailed to me. I will always treasure it and hold it dear to my heart. I've read it so many times that the edges are frayed.

My Dearest Kree,

Don't hate me, baby girl; I don't think I could live with that. I know I hurt you deeply, but I never meant for that to happen. Please believe me. You deserved so much more from me. You came into my life and gave me a second chance at love. Many people never get the first chance at love. But you—you literally unthawed my heart. I saw you that night in the club and I knew . . . you were the one I could love.

I know you always thought you played second fiddle to my first marriage. But believe me, I always loved you for you. My perfect little wife who loved me with everything she had to give. Always in my corner supporting, encouraging, and taking care of me with a smile. I loved you, Kree, and always will. That will never change. Our love was a different love from the one I shared with Mia, but it wasn't any less.

I didn't mean to hurt you, baby, and make you cry. Please forgive me. Please. Don't worry; I won't bother you anymore. You're still young. Find someone who will love you the way you deserve to be loved, and appreciate your many talents and beauty. You will forever be in my heart.

Love always,

Brice

Fresh tears escaped my eyes and I quickly wiped them away with the back of my hand. I clutched the letter in my left hand as I gently caressed my stomach and the life growing inside of me. Brice's baby. I fell asleep, thinking of how things could have been so different. We could have been so happy. So very happy.

Epilogue

Kree

One year later

I guess I need to tie up a few loose ends. I wish I could say that everyone lived happily ever after, but we all know that only happens in fairy tales. Real life is never so convenient, neat or simple.

Let's see. Where do I begin? Mia and Christian. Almost a year after Brice's death, they found their way back to each other. It was a slow, gradual process, but their love is real and true; it was only a matter of time. True love can't be separated. Mia is a mature, wiser woman, and their marriage is stronger than ever. Solid. Whenever I see them, they are all smiles. They're truly happy and will be fine. Just fine. In their case, love did conquer all.

Amazingly, we are all friends now. This didn't happen overnight; it was a slow process as well. A lot of people would say I'm crazy to be friends with a woman who had an affair with my husband. But my connection to Mia runs so much deeper . . . So they can say whatever they please. I've forgiven Mia. Most important, Mia has forgiven herself. Yes, we are a weird li'l extended family, with our share of secrets, misdeeds and ties.

My brother, Miles, and his wife relocated to Atlanta to help me run the security business. So, yes, Security Unlimited, Inc., is up and running. In fact, we just got two new contracts. Business couldn't be better. We are making Brice's dream a reality.

Christian was also brought in as a partner, and he and Miles are quickly becoming great friends. Christian is an amazing man. I respect and admire him so much. Maybe when I'm ready to enter the dating arena (in another hundred years), I'll be lucky enough to meet someone like him. What else? As for me, I'm still teaching dance to six- to twelve-year olds at Spelman's in my spare time, and loving it.

Last, but certainly not least, my biggest and greatest news is that Brice Christian Matthew II was born healthy and happy, weighing eight pounds, and twenty-two inches long. He looks just like his father, and I already love him with all my being. When he's older, I'm going to tell him all about Brice—the good, the bad and the ugly. He'll know about his father and won't make the same mistakes Brice did. My son is my savior and keeps me sane.

As strange as it may sound, sometimes I feel Brice looking down upon us, smiling. And I smile back. I feel myself slowly healing and I rejoice in it.

Moms has been in town playing the doting grandmother. Brice Junior, or B.J. as we call him, can't even cry without her picking him up, spoiling him already. Oddly enough, she and Mia's mom have been hanging tight. Moms doesn't know all the details of what truly happened. Mia's mom does! That's for the best. She likes Atlanta so much that she's thinking about moving here. Watch out, Hotlanta!

I take B.J. over to Vivica's at least once a week. He puts a big smile on her face. We lost Brice's dad in the spring. He fought a good fight, but in the end he passed away quietly in his sleep in his own bed. Christian helps out over there as much as he can. Vivica insists on inviting us to dinner almost every Sunday—our entire extended family.

Life is moving on. That's the beauty of life. It's a continuous cycle of death and birth, never ending. I still have my good and bad days, but my heart will go on. I think of Brice often. I loved him, I can't deny it, and I know he loved me in his own way. But I'm letting go of the past. I learned my lesson from Mia. The past has no place in the present if you want to move forward into the future. I think we have all grown in ways we would have never imagined. As Mother would say, "Child, what doesn't kill you only makes you stronger."

Electa Rome Parks currently lives outside Atlanta, Georgia, with her husband, Nelson, and their two children. With a BA degree in marketing, she is presently working on her next novel and fulfilling her passion as a writer.

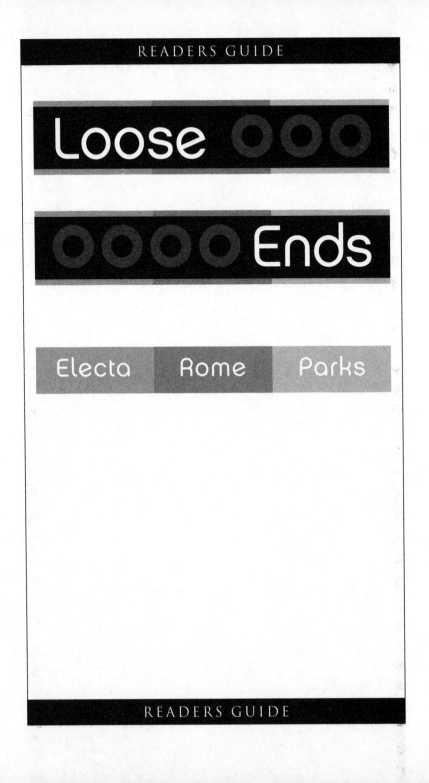

Loose Ends

Electa   Rome   Parks

A CONVERSATION WITH
ELECTA ROME PARKS

Q. What can you tell your readers about Electa Rome Parks?

A. Umm, that's a hard question. It's not easy to define or describe oneself in a condensed version, but I'll try. I was born and
raised in Georgia. So, yes, I'm a true Georgia peach even though
I lived in Chicago and North Carolina for many years. Basically,
I'm just your average, down-to-earth, wife and mother of two
who has a great passion for writing and reading. Honestly, I
don't think I could live without books and the written word.
I've found that a pen to paper is a powerful tool!

Let's see, what else can I divulge about myself and keep you
interested (smile)? Believe it or not, I'm actually kinda quiet and
laid-back. I can be moody and oversensitive (Pisces trait). So . . .
be careful what you say about *Loose Ends* because I'm sensitive
about my stuff (LOL).

I have a very vivid imagination that is evident in my books,
and I believe in a lot of theories that most people would think
bizarre. Let's just say I absolutely love *X-Files* and the entire
concept of spirits, guardian angels and karma. I once had a palm
reader tell me I was a writer in another life and that's why writing validates and elevates me to be in complete sync with my
spirit. I thought that was so deep and so unbelievably true.

Bottom line, anyone who truly knows me will state that I'm real. I'm very approachable and have a genuinely caring nature (another Pisces trait). I have my "few" imperfections and struggles just like the next person. However, I believe in order to really get in touch with our true spirit, we need to discover our gifts. I feel that we are all born into the world with a special gift, and I've found mine. That brings me great joy!

What else? I pretty much suck at any sport, my favorite color is purple, I've never weighed more than 112 pounds my entire life, my all-time favorite movie is a toss between *Soul Food* and *The Best Man* and I have tons of stories to share with my readers.

Q. Who has been your writing inspiration?

A. I have a great love and admiration for contemporary writers such as Terry McMillan, Eric Jerome Dickey, Bebe Moore Campbell, E. Lynn Harris, Kimberla Lawson Roby, etc., to name a few. For me, reading and writing go hand in hand. I read for entertainment, to relax and unwind, to take a minivacation for 250 pages or so. Through reading I travel to new places and meet new and interesting people without ever leaving the comfort of my home. Amazing. So I tend to write that way. I like for my readers to feel I'm letting them in on some juicy gossip and that my characters are talking directly to them. I'm a very emotional person and my characters tend to be.

Additionally, contemporary writers were the first ones to inspire me to follow my dreams. I vividly remember that the first time I read *Disappearing Acts,* I was in absolute, undeniable awe. I discovered characters that looked like me, talked like me, acted like me, and I savored each and every word like a fine gourmet dinner. I felt the characters' pain, triumphs and joy because I could relate. I didn't want that novel to end. It was with true sadness that I read the last page. From that point it was on; I devoured any African American fiction I could get my hands on; I was addicted. To this day, I'm still addicted.

If I want to be really deep and philosophical for a few days, I read Toni Morrison, Alice Walker or Gloria Naylor. They always elevate my spirit and mind to a higher plane. Their words soothe my soul with their wisdom and insight. I've enjoyed the classics as well with such writers as Zora Neale Hurston, Ralph Ellison and James Baldwin.

Additionally, I adore Stephen King and Dean Koontz because I'm a big supernatural/horror fan.

Q. Describe your writing style.

A. (LOL) There is no name or definition to define my writing style; it's pretty unorthodox. To put it simply, I go with the flow. I come up with a general story line in my head, and then I simply sit down in front of my PC and start typing. I don't believe in outlines, or at least I can't function in a writing environment with one.

When I'm writing, I have no idea what my beginning, middle or ending is. However, I know my characters like the back of my hand. I could tell you what they got for their twelfth birthdays down to what they ate for lunch two weeks ago. In writing, I let my characters talk to me and dictate their story. Sometimes we fight about how a certain scene should play out, but in the long run, they win. Yes, it's weird, but true.

Q. What type of atmosphere do you require to write?

A. When I really get into a writing project, it doesn't matter what type of atmosphere I surround myself with. The words will flow naturally.

A lot of times I mentally write my chapters when I'm driving. I can drive, zone out mentally (without causing an accident) and come up with great dialogue and an additional chapter or two. When I arrive home, I swiftly run to my PC and simply type it up before I forget. So it's like I'm writing down what I saw at a movie or play, with great detail included.

If I had to name a preference, I prefer a somewhat quiet, relaxing, peaceful atmosphere.

Q. How long did it take you to complete Loose Ends?

A. I'll be the first to admit, I'm not the most disciplined writer; however, I'm working on it. I'm not going to lie (LOL). Sometimes I can be lazy, and no matter how loudly my characters are calling me back to my PC to bring their story to fruition, sleep is screaming louder and there's a bed with my name written on it.

But, in my defense, until recently I was employed full-time in communications, and I'm a wife and mother of two children who keep me running ragged. However, I digress. To answer your question, it took me approximately eight months to complete *Loose Ends.*

Q. What were the happiest moments you have experienced while writing your latest book?

A. My happiest moments were just seeing the story line come together and unfold before my eyes. Each new page, each new chapter brought revelations my way. *Loose Ends* is the follow-up or continuation to my first novel, *The Ties That Bind*. So writing *Loose Ends* was like welcoming long-lost friends back into the fold. It felt exhilarating and right and good. Writing *Loose Ends* was like being reunited with family that I hadn't seen in a while. I enjoyed having Brice, Mia, Kree and Christian back in my life again.

The saddest moment was when I wrote the last sentence; I was depressed for weeks.

Q. What has been the most gratifying part of being an author?

A. Hands down, the most gratifying part of being an author has been meeting and greeting new and interesting readers who are embracing my stories and e-mailing me and writing me and meeting me at signings and telling me how much they've enjoyed my books! We talk about my characters like they are old friends. No matter how many times I've experienced that, it always makes my day. Puts a big Kool-Aid smile on my face (LOL).

Their (the readers') feedback and reactions totally validates that my craft is a gift from God! If I can touch a number of people with my stories or even if I only entertain them and they don't walk away with a life lesson, then I've still done my job.

As you know, my stories are typically relationship based, very drama filled, with an ounce of spice thrown in—well, maybe a pound of spice thrown in—and they usually cover a topical issue that is prevalent in today's society. Believe me, I have so many characters screaming inside my head, waiting to tell their story, that I feel like the lady from the movie *Sybil* (LOL). So, bottom line, I pray and claim that my readership base will continue to grow and I'll have wonderful opportunities to meet many more fans.

Q. Where do you see yourself as a writer ten years from now?

A. It's all about continuing to elevate myself to the next level. There's always room for growth and improvement. Ten years from now, I'd love to see myself as a full-time writer entertaining my readers with fabulous, refreshing, dramatic stories of love, life and relationships. It's not about the money; it's all about the passion and joy you feel with each and every heartfelt word that turns into a sentence, then a paragraph, and eventually a completed novel. Being a writer is like being a creator of life . . . like giving birth. What can be better than that?

Q. How can readers get in contact with you?

A. My readers can keep abreast of my writing career through my Web site at www.electaromeparks.com. And please, readers, drop me a line, give me some feedback (remember I'm sensitive now), just holla at a sista at novelideal@aol.com.

QUESTIONS FOR DISCUSSION

1. Even though it is five years later, why do you feel Mia is having nightmares about Brice? Do you feel she has moved on with her life? Or is closure needed?

2. Why is it so important for Christian to reunite with Brice? Are Christian's reasons totally selfish? Realistically, can Christian and Brice's relationship/friendship ever be the same?

3. Should Mia stand her ground and not give in and agree to the reunion?

4. Why does Brice feel the need to reunite with Christian? With Mia?

5. What is the significance of Mia and Kree looking very similar in physical appearance?

6. Is it possible for Mia to still love a man who physically abused her? If so, why and how?

7. Has Brice changed at all in his new marriage to Kree? Does he want to change?

8. Even though Mia is happy with Christian and has the perfect life, why did she risk it all to sleep with Brice? Is it possible for one person to have that much power over another person?

9. Who is stronger, Mia or Kree? What do you think of Mia and Kree in the beginning of the story? At the end?

10. Do you feel that Brice intentionally sets out to seduce Mia or, as he says, "it just happened"?

11. Do you feel Brice commits suicide or is it a tragic accident?

12. Will Mia and Christian's marriage become even stronger now? Or will Christian never be able to trust Mia? Is Christian partly to blame for what happened?

13. It's five years after the story ends: What are Mia, Christian and Kree up to?